WORLD LITERATURE
IN TRANSLATION

FEDERIGO TOZZI

GHISOLA

Translated with an Afterword by
CHARLES KLOPP

Conclusion by
GIOSE RIMANELLI

GARLAND PUBLISHING, INC.
NEW YORK & LONDON 1990

Library of Congress Cataloging-in-Publication Data

Tozzi, Federigo, 1883–1920.
  [Con gli occhi chiusi. English]
  Ghisola/Federigo Tozzi; translated with an afterword by Charles Klopp
  p. cm. (The Garland library of world literature in translation: v. 18)
  Translation of: Con gli occhi chiusi
  ISBN 0-8240-3313-2
  I. Title. II. Series
PQ4843.08C613 1989
853.912—dc20 89-23396

Printed on acid-free, 250-year-life paper
Manufactured in the United States of America

GHISOLA
Con gli occhi chiusi

Domenico Rosi, the restaurant owner, had stayed behind after the cooks and waiters had gone home. In the light of a guttering candle he was hurriedly counting up the day's take. When he came to two fifty-lira notes, he rubbed the bills between his fingers, staring at them for a while before folding them up and putting them into his yellow leather wallet. Then, his mouth close to the flame, he blew out the candle. Had more candle been left, he would have counted the money in his wife's drawer too. Instead, he locked the door, pushing it with his knee afterwards to make sure he had locked it properly. He lived almost right across the street from the restaurant.

Even though he had been in the business for thirty years, he could still remember his very first profits, and the memories that he could feel nudging inside him each evening were as satisfying as a good day's take.

His own restaurant! Sometimes, when he talked about it, he would slap the wall in pride and satisfaction.

Even though he had lived in town for quite a while, he was still basically a peasant, perfectly ready to use his fists to settle a slur on his honesty. In his view, God had decided to look after him and help him get rich. But people were so jealous that he wanted to get still richer. There were plenty of people who would have done anything to ruin him!

His four sisters and three brothers were still poor; they still lived in Civitella in the Maremma in a chipped stone house in the middle of the boar-infested woods. The stairs were made from rocks taken from the riverbed and wobbled beneath your feet; the windows looked out onto a mountain of marl so close and steep it seemed the house lay under it and one day the mountain would fall and crush it. Whenever Rosi thought about that narrow little town, it was like about something that no longer existed—or existed only for other people. His childhood memories were as worthless as the theaters and newspaper pictures he despised and hated: fine nonsense for people who were lazy or had money to waste. The same went for smoking. No one had ever seen him at the theater, or with a cigar in his mouth! He was too clever for that!

He was only twenty and had just arrived in Siena when he married Anna—a pretty orphan with no dowry, younger than he was—and opened *The Blue Fish*, a restaurant that had grown to one of the best in the city.

Their son Pietro was almost fourteen. Before him there had been seven others, but they had all died shortly after coming home from the wet nurse. They sent Pietro to the nearest school, a seminary where he had fallen behind because of his health and was one of the external students. That is, he took his classes with the seminarians but lived at home and was excused from the dress regulations. The birth before Pietro's had left Anna with convulsions. She had also suffered for some time from hysteria: a sickness that Domenico thought was hilarious and treated as a joke with a point he couldn't quite fathom. But he found it irritating and almost a personal affront when laughing didn't help and the druggist had a bill that had to be paid.

Anna was a quiet person but crazy about him. When she finally discovered after years of marriage that he was betraying her, she felt they were pulling with both hands at her heart while she grew ugly and prematurely old. Though tears welled up in her eyes at the thought, there was no one she could talk to about this. For even though she was very polite, she did not want to get entangled in friendships. Still, sometimes her forbearance was so great it almost choked her as tears coursed down on her upper lip and she sniffed at her aromatic vinegar.

She had the plumpish face of an overweight woman and no one understood the sudden rages that exposed her excitable but fundamentally innocuous character. Fits like hers were like the outbreaks of a tormented animal. Everybody laughs, in fact, when a chicken runs round with its throat slit or a rabbit squeaks and shows its claws!

Both Anna and Domenico wanted an heir. Their dead children, therefore, had turned into symbols of unsuccessful attempts that had been willed so by destiny. But Anna loved Pietro with a superstitious passion. Even though she liked to keep him close, she couldn't manage to show him much tenderness. When Pietro went to sleep on her shoulder, she never knew when to call Rebecca, his old wet nurse who worked for them now and was responsible for the wine cellar, and have her put the child to bed.

At moments like these Domenico would bellow from the bustle and excitement of the kitchen where he was working: "Are you still lugging that weight around?"

Since she didn't want him to come and take Pietro in his bare forearms, she would wake the child and send him to bed. The next night she would try harder to make him mind. "Get away," she would whisper. "You're bothering me."

But Pietro paid no attention. Eyes heavy with sleep, he would squeeze next to the arm of the chair and take her hand. Since she had to make change for the waiters and wave to the customers coming and going, Anna would pull her hand away. The restaurant was busy until late at night. Although the work excited her too, by midnight everyone was exhausted and ready for bed. If there was still someone sitting at one of the tables, they would put out the lights in the other rooms, one by one. The waiters would take off their jackets and the cooks would put on fresh aprons. In such moments of anticipation and rest, Anna would do some mending or simple embroidery—nothing fancy but something that did save money. She had started as a waitress when very young and had never had time for much education. But she knew how to write and had learned so well from experience that she never made a mistake figuring the customers' bills.

She made sure that everything was in order: the plates and bowls on top of the old bread-chest, the bread and wine flasks in the sideboard. And she knew how to handle the tradesmen. She picked out the lemons herself, though with Domenico watching so carefully it made her proud and happy. If the fruitseller did manage to slip her a lemon with a thick or discolored rind, Domenico would push it under his nose and make him take it back.

When she could, Anna went to bed half an hour before he did. One night Domenico grabbed a drunken mechanic who had refused to leave, yanking him right out of his chair and into the street. The man opened his knife and charged, but Domenico jumped aside and the waiters got in between them. Anna, who was standing right there with that same woolen shawl she always wore on her head, was so upset that her convulsions got stronger and more frequent. As treatment, the doctor prescribed that she spend as much time as she could at Poggio a' Meli, the farm they had just bought. But since she couldn't be away from the restaurant on market day, she came back to Siena on Saturdays, bringing Pietro and Rebecca with her. Although Domenico slept in the city, he got into his two-seater buggy each morning and brought his wife a basket of food for the next day, holding it tight in his knees so it wouldn't tip over.

Poggio a' Meli, or Apple-Tree Hill, lies outside Porta Camollia on the lonely road that runs from Palazzo dei Diavoli to just beyond the Poggio al Vento Convent. The one-story house was old and had been repainted red; the wine shed was attached to it and there were rooms for the farmhands over the barn. Domenico liked the red color but Anna—and several of her friends agreed with her—would have picked either light blue or canary yellow.

The farm yard was right in front of the house with the well to one side and a circular arbor where Domenico kept a dozen tubs of lemon trees in good weather—the only real extravagance in the whole garden. Even if these were an expense that gave him very little return, he made a great fuss over them. More often than not, if the mood were on him, he wouldn't let Pietro even touch them.

The farm was only a few acres, with a hedge of Christ-thorn and hawthorn on the street side, one tiny, well-tilled level field, and the rest hillside sloping down to the foot of another little hill beneath the Porta Camollia wall.

Large, black oaks mixed with some tall walnuts ran along the property line; down in the bottom land, where the water was, there were willows and vegetable gardens. From the farmyard you could see Siena.

After mass on the last Sunday of the month the farmhands would come to the restaurant and Rosi would pay them as they made their marks as best they could on the revenue seals. Then he would discuss the work with them, letting them know what he wanted done. He was never satisfied and always threatened to fire them. Then he would give them their next day's orders—more loudly this time— and send them away. Since customers would be starting to arrive by then, he would roll up his sleeves and go into the kitchen. He usually ate breakfast while paying them off.

Even though the farm was small and had the buildings arranged that way, it was very pretty. There was something about it that made you feel you wanted to stay for a while: the line of five cypresses behind the low farmyard wall, and then nothing but olive and fruit trees. "If it were any bigger, it wouldn't be as nice," someone said once after inspecting it a couple of times. The dirt was dark red in the one level field; the other fields were made of hard yellowish clay. In spring, except for where it had been plowed or spaded, the land turned a hundred different greens that took a long time to fade in the autumn.

At certain hours of the morning there would be Capuchins passing while peasants in their carts were always going by. Thursdays, toward noon, there would be beggars on their way for some soup at the convent. And in the fall there would be families of vacationers and out-of-towners from a boardinghouse; they would stay out into the evening. Nice Sundays there might be a group of friends out singing after drinks in the restaurants and wine-shops beyond the walls.

The road out there is level and mostly quite narrow, with scattered villas and other farms, and then oaks, holm oaks, chestnuts, wooden gates, and pruned hedges. But there are nicer villas too that run out to the Marciano church and the clump of hills toward Mount Amiata and the Maremma.

When a new owner who is not a fool takes over a farm, he is sure to change it in some way that will be immediately apparent to those who understand and evident later to those who don't. Rosi wasted no time changing Poggio a' Meli. When the blossoms from his newly planted peach and almond trees blew into the middle of the road, he would rein in his horse, look up, and swear at the branches with nothing but leaves on them. Then he would whip Toppa, who was jumping up and down barking with happiness at his arrival. He used to walk for hours in the vine rows, checking for disease while one of the hands followed behind and was certain to tell him that whatever went wrong wasn't their fault. If a vine did seem badly tied or poorly staked, he would call for another wythe and redo the job on the spot.

Pruning the olive trees caused endless arguments. Though he put the ladder wherever he wanted, he was too heavy to climb up himself and had to indicate from the ground which branches he wanted them to trim.

When they were spading he would sometimes show them how to get the best cut.

During grape harvest he did the washing and rinsing of the casks and barrels himself and kept an eye on the spout of the wine tun too.

Since it made no difference to Domenico, and Anna was by now fond of Rebecca—a woman who had been made pregnant by a man who then refused to marry her—Giacco and Masa, Rebecca's elderly parents, were taken on at Poggio a' Meli. They were poor and all their other daughters were married and gone. So after a year or two they asked the master if it was all right for Ghisola, a grand-child from Radda and the daughter of one of Rebecca's sisters, to come and live with them.

Giacco and Masa never threw out so much as half a rusty nail. Giacco's green corduroy trousers were so covered with patches that you could only see a few strips of the original material. The hand-kerchief on Masa's head was one she had bought as a young girl.

Masa could never get the meals ready on time. Giacco, his eyes fixed on her, would fly into a rage and start to swear while she got rattled and took even longer. What a sight! After pouring a thread of oil that was as thin as a needle point from the tin jug, she would carefully wipe the spout and lick the opening a couple of times and then put the jug back in the bread chest. By then the oil in the pan would be ready and she would toss in some garlic and chopped on-ion. When the garlic was toasted and yellow, she would pour the mixture into a pot of salted water and put the pot back on the fire while she sliced bread, pulling on the knife with both hands and holding the loaf against her chest. Toppa, the watch dog, made the crumbs disappear just as fast as they fell but Masa—who wanted the crumbs for the chickens—would get upset and try to shove him away with her foot.

Giacco would wash up in a battered copper basin as soon as he came in, then sit and rub his face with his stubby, callused fingers.

Finally Masa would pour the water over the sliced bread while Ghisola brought the salt and pepper packets, getting a scolding when she came to the table because she had rubbed her shoulder against the wall when she crossed the room.

Giacco's mind was still on the calf butting his shoulder when he had filled its feedtrough with hay. "Can't you see you're getting hair all over me?" he had said as he pushed it away.

"Put the animal's mash on the fire before you sit down," he said to his wife. "You always pretend you can't remember what you have to do."

Now that his chores were done, he felt affectionate about those friendly butts in the barn where the calf's breath was as warm and damp as his own sweat. He ate in silence thinking about it.

Sometimes Anna would knock at their door. When she did, all three of them would jump to their feet. "It's the mistress. Hurry and open it. What are you waiting for?"

Pietro didn't get to see Poggio a' Meli for one whole winter, hearing only what his father said to the customers about it. There were new grape vines, new fruit trees ready for planting, a heavier wheat sowing, and a new wine that was almost transparent, tasted of sulphur, and burned the stomach.

Sometimes Ghisola would turn up at the restaurant and stand in silence next to her Aunt Rebecca while he stared at her without moving. But it seemed they hardly knew each other and he didn't like this at all.

Toward June, after a couple of bouts of mild fever, he went back with his mother to the country. Since the house was kept closed several months of the year, it always smelled of mice and mortar when they got there and they had to use force to turn the keys in the locks. This hurt their hands and they called Giacco to do it the first time; Masa's job was to clean the dust and cobwebs from the rooms.

Ghisola helped too, though she was not allowed to touch anything breakable.

The first day he was there Pietro had a seizure that left him unconscious and with his glands swollen and aching behind his ears.

He liked to tear up all the plantings he could get his hands on, rip the new shoots off the grape vines, or hit a tree with a vine-stake until the bark came off. He pulled the legs and wings from crickets and then stuck them on a pin. When a cloud came over the sky he would stare at it after it had gone—almost hoping another would arrive.

Finally, without thunder, the rain arrived and the water gushed in endless streams from the downspouts. When the clouds lifted, rays of light played over the hills where some more rain was weaving a veil so fine that the wind could easily have ripped it away. Then, as if waiting for just such a moment, the rainbow burst open.

After dinner Anna invited Masa and the other farm wives into the house; they came in stumbling at every step.

"Sit down."

"But mistress," they would answer, "are you sure we're not too much trouble for you?"

"Sit down, I tell you."

Though Anna liked to give orders and play the mistress, she was also genuinely fond of these women.

Ghisola sat still and serious watching the others. Pietro was supposed to be studying. He stared at the part in her hair, hair that was combed so tight it looked like hemp on a reel, then looked away until his mother told her to go to the next room for another skein of wool. Jumping to do as she was told, she lurched forward like a huge marionette and then hunched down again, her feet on the rung of the chair and her eyes glued to the mistress' crocheting.

When she noticed this, Anna leaned back and held up her hands, "Look, this is how you hold the hook, pick up the yarn . . . then turn it over here . . . and pick it up again. It's easy."

"My, she's clever!" said Orsola, who hadn't understood anything and who had a nose that was all red from broken blood vessels.

"Would you like to learn how?" Masa asked her granddaughter.

"Ghisola is young and has the right fingers for such work, but ours won't even bend anymore," said Orsola, scratching her head with a darning needle.

"And we can't see well either," added Adele, who had the worst eyesight.

"What can we do? Cook a little bread-soup for our men. And not cook it very well either!"

After they all laughed, Masa exclaimed, "Look what delicate fingers the mistress has! It just doesn't seem possible!"

Anna blushed, dropped her crocheting, and put one of her hands under the light on the table, turning it so they could see both sides. Her hand was small and plump with short, puffy nails.

Even though Pietro was paying careful attention, the people around him seemed like figures in his dreams. When she asked him something, his mother had to repeat it two or three times.

"How can you be so absentminded? Though you still keep track of what we're saying!"

Pietro was afraid to answer and could feel a strange apprehension. He couldn't shake off that familiar, irresistible dread and felt caught in a feeling of estrangement that sometimes gave him terrible comfort. Getting up from his chair, he went over to the sofa where at last he felt sleepy and began to nod. At a signal from her mistress, Ghisola took her darning needle and went over and pricked him on the hand to get him to move. At first, sunk in that crushing abyss, Pietro pretended not to feel it. Then, his eyes still shut, he slapped her in the face. For now he realized with a sharp pang that Ghisola too was part of that harsh reality so inferior to his dream world.

"You hurt me!"

His face had gone a sickly white and he was much less calm. To prevent him from crying, Anna sent the girl home early. Ghisola was insulted as well as frightened and quickly slipped away.

The rain, which had started again after the sunset, rattled quietly among the lightning bugs that had refused to budge.

Some of these were clinging motionless to the wheat stalks where you could see their unblinking lights holding steady beneath the raindrops' buffeting.

Pietro was sleepy and his eyes kept closing as he let them take off his clothes. Once he was in bed, his mother looked at him. "You haven't said so much as an 'Avemaria' for three nights!" she said. "Cross yourself!"

If he hadn't been so sleepy, he would have done it. But sensing that the sign of the cross was already on his body, and remembering with voluptuousness what he had said to Ghisola, he did move his arm, though not all the way to his forehead. As he went to sleep he could see his mother moving shadow-like past his bed to kiss him goodnight.

"At least say good night!"

But by the time she had put his socks and underpants under the pillow and went out, blocking the light with her body, he was fast asleep.

At midnight he woke up. He could hear a nightingale—in the oaks by the farmyard, perhaps. The call seemed a message that the bird's mate was answering in the distance. He couldn't help listening to both birds for a long time, imagining that Ghisola was outside trying to catch them. And he wondered why all the people and things around him were never more than a heavy wavering nightmare.

As he dreamed, he felt how wicked he was and seemed to be cursing the song.

Masa had knocked over the oil lamp after it came loose from the nail in the wall. Now she was waiting for bad luck to arrive.

Though the fire in the hearth where she was sitting had gone out, the stones were still warm. She wrung her hands under her skirt stuffed between her thighs, rubbed her eyebrows, and massaged the huge lump in her stomach.

Though she didn't want to talk about it, when she heard Carlo's wife Orsola going by, she called out to her. "Do you know what I've done?"

"No. What have you done?"

Masa moved her lips without answering.

"Tell me. What are you waiting for? Why did you call me?"

"I've spilled the oil."

"Are you joking?"

"I'm not like you. I don't joke about such things."

"Neither do I, as far as that goes. Better watch out."

Masa could have slapped her. Orsola had her head down and was thinking of the bad luck in store for her.

"And there's nothing I can think of that I've done wrong."

"It doesn't make any difference what you've done, you know.

Do you remember that time when the fox tore up the brood-hen I had forgotten to lock in? I'd spilled the oil that time. If that wasn't enough, my husband almost gave me a beating as well!"

Masa rubbed the palm of her hand against her cheek and Orsola scratched at her chest, moving the whole front of her jacket with her fist.

"Don't worry about it," she said. "But come and tell me what happens; I'm curious to know." And she left.

Just to be sure they weren't lying dead in the fields, Masa went out to meet Giacco and Ghisola. But she was in no mood for a scolding and didn't tell Giacco about it. But when Ghisola heard, she was so superstitiously afraid that she wouldn't go into her room to change her apron in the dark.

Instead, she picked up the nest with the five baby sparrows that she had taken from a poplar tree she had climbed. Holding it on her knee, she started to stuff bread crumbs into the open mouths. Although she wanted to raise the little birds, she could also feel the desire to kill them: a thought that terrified and excited her. One was blinking its eyes, another raising its wings and toppling over, and another kept chirping constantly.

In the end, she crushed their heads between her fingers and threw them into the frying pan. Masa, who refused to even taste them, was looking imploringly at the sooty crucifix and trying to keep from thinking about it. Afterwards she sat down, shook her head, and then looked out through the doorway.

Toppa came in and dived under the table. Banging his tail against the jute tablecloth, he sniffed each of the chairs before going back out.

Grandmother and granddaughter looked each other in the eye. What was meant by the circle he had made in the room?

But the bad luck never did arrive. "The danger's over now," Orsola said to Masa after dinner.

"She has all the luck," she thought jealously, after checking that the oil really had been spilled.

Ghisola was standing in the window spitting at intervals at something she couldn't quite see in the dark. Then she looked at the sky where more and more stars were appearing.

A moist strip of inky clouds neatly divided the dark blue sky from a horizon made radiant by the last rays of the setting sun. In the olive trees the leaves were like a single bolt of cloth draped across the open branches.

The cypresses in the farmyard were black.

Gnats and moths brushed her forehead as the warm stench of the barn beneath her mingled with an unknown fragrance.

In a peach tree with soft and sticky flowers a cicada screamed as if caught in a dream.

Flour! Masa was well aware of the meaning and value of flour— flour that sticks to your fingers and is locked in the bread-chest with a reverence bordering on fanaticism. When she ate sliced bread she seemed like a bumpkin who has never had cake in his mouth and is afraid of finishing it up too soon. Sitting with one leg crossed, she would bite it carefully into pieces, using her whole mouth except for her lips. Then she would swallow, her eyes fixed on the slice still clutched in her fingers.

The flour was her, was her entire family. "Aren't we made out of bread too?" Giacco used to say.

When he plunged his bare arm into the wheat sack to check that it hadn't heated up and gone bad, every single grain seemed to be trying to stick to him.

"Any bugs in it?" Masa would ask.

"If there are, you'd be better off with a busted rib."

Masa turned red, but was glad too.

Agostino, the son of a horsedealer who owned two farms next to Poggio a' Meli, wanted Pietro to stop paying so much attention to Ghisola. This was due to that egotism that in young people is so similar to jealousy, though he also recognized that he ought to despise Pietro for his ingenuous kindness, pity him in fact for having such a weakness.

Ghisola did make the young master feel embarrassed and uncomfortable. He wished he were strong too and tried to persuade himself it was better to have Agostino for a friend than Ghisola.

Whenever he was with him he took the weaker part and did what he was told, even trying to figure out what the other boy was thinking but not telling him. Sometimes he would pick up a stone Agostino had chosen with a glance and wanted to throw at the next bird he saw in a roadside tree. How the wind billowed Agostino's unbuttoned shirt! Why wasn't his own shirt, why weren't his wrists, his eyebrows, his ears like Agostino's? And when he tried to imitate his nonchalant manners, why did he lose his nerve and get short of breath and worry he was going to drive his friend into one of those rages that made him tremble? Why couldn't he meet his impenetrably clear gaze when Agostino was angry and he was stumbling for answers to his questions? That gaze frightened him the same way he was frightened once when under his feet he unexpectedly discovered a spring.

Agostino had a stubby baby nose that was covered with freckles. But his hands were shapely and his neck would have looked good on a beautiful woman. His conversations with Ghisola, which consisted entirely of meaningless phrases that only the two of them knew about and understood, excited emotions in Pietro that he never would have dreamed of by himself. But he loved to listen to them! He even thought he was learning something.

When she said those things only she could say, Ghisola smiled so pleasantly that Pietro went weak with desire and wanted to know more—the jingles she sang, for example. But he couldn't even sing and was embarrassed. Sometimes, to keep her from laughing, he would do something mean on purpose.

Ghisola's tranquil face looked weak and insignificant under her big straw hat that slumped over one ear. The hat was decorated with a worn satin ribbon and two rosettes that Anna had discarded. In her badly mended petticoat she seemed extremely homely, even stupid.

Some people don't ever expect anything from anybody and always give up right away. Since no one respects them, it appears that you can treat them any way you please. This is why they don't want to get involved with anything that concerns other people. If someone falls in love with them, they don't try to change, but insist on finding out what is required of them. When they do find out, they refuse to do it.

When Masa rapped her knuckles against Ghisola's forehead and asked, "What is it that you've got in there?" Ghisola would answer exasperated, "What do you care? What do you know about it?"

She found it both pleasing and irritating to think that her face upset people. She never said anything when other people were talking because she assumed they were talking about her. Nothing interested her; if she obeyed Masa and the master and mistress, it was because without them, she wouldn't have known even to do her darning. She hated to admit that anything existed outside of her self.

She would often sit outside on the stairs and sometimes seemed to be holding long talks with them.

She didn't dare have ideas of her own since she knew full well that too many of those she did have were not the right ones. So too, when she came into the restaurant, she didn't dare ask for the scrumptious things she saw: things that made her face hot and her head swim like the overheated room that she wasn't used to either.

But deep inside her she had a presentiment of a life that made her dizzy just the way others are dizzied by ideas of wealth and luxury.

It was with Ghisola that Pietro first felt tender emotions and he was grateful to her for them. He stared in amazement at a flower he wanted, picking and discarding it afterwards because he didn't dare present it to her. He didn't quite believe what was happening, but somehow felt diminished. How suddenly and violently nature had turned mysterious. It was enough to drive you crazy!

He had spent time face down on the ground with his arms encircling a baby chick he wanted to keep close! He had helped ants by removing a stick that they had been trying first hesitantly and then frantically to cross—staggering the whole time under impossible burdens that knocked them topsy-turvy! He would cradle ladybugs in his hand, scolding them when they flew away!

Even though he wanted to control his fits of depression, he couldn't help brooding. Sometimes he would suddenly be wrenched out of such a mood, only to fall back into a confused and murky feeling that always seemed just on the verge of going away. And his mind would seem to swell up to such proportions that his thoughts and the sudden reverberations they made were completely lost as if in an outsized room. How many times had he just given up to the ceaseless images bombarding him! Though at first he seemed to have a grip on his consciousness, it kept on slipping away from him in a seesaw movement that made him feel as if he had just had an attack of dizziness.

Sometimes he would think he was in school and all of a sudden a bass drum came into the room. He would want to laugh so much that he would be terrified and choke and scream from his nightmare. Anna would think he was sick and feel his forehead. "Do you have a fever?" she would ask.

"No! No!" he would shriek. "Leave me alone!"

A year had gone by since the night of the nightingales, a year like all the others: the customers and the restaurant, the farm hands and Poggio a' Meli.

By springtime Domenico wanted to be ready for the bumper harvest he was expecting. So, almost as if to make up for all his hard work at the restaurant, he went out to the farm more often. And since the weather was fine, he always took Pietro along. It did the boy good; maybe now he'd stop getting sick so much!

He wanted him to go into the fields and check the vine pruning and everything else the same way he did. But Pietro acted as if he had gone deaf and blind. So Domenico would call one of the women who had just come in with a bundle of fresh fodder or some weeds pulled from the plowed field and have her take him back to the farmyard.

Unconsciously, Pietro always imitated Ghisola. One day he was waiting for his father, sitting on Giacco's steps where she always played. Masa was sweeping with a broom attached to an old umbrella handle; the dust she was raising was so thick he could taste it.

"Get up," the old woman told him.

When he refused to budge, she stopped sweeping.

Among the bits of multicolored trash, tangles of hair, and broken boxes lay a doll made out of a wooden spoon with a piece of white cloth wrapped around it. Pietro wanted to rescue it and stood up. At that the old woman saw her chance and pushed the sweepings out the door. And for that instant the doll, which was lying face down, suddenly seemed so alive that Pietro refused to touch it. When Ghisola came back from the fields and saw it there with the sweepings, she said nothing since her grandmother had been trying for a long time to get her to throw it out. But she looked like she was going to burst into tears.

"Are you still fussing about that thing?" Masa shouted at her.

Thinking to tease her, Pietro pushed the doll down into the mud with his foot. Then, suddenly pale and with his heart pounding in terror that it would come back to the surface, he began to stomp on it furiously.

Ghisola was watching from the doorway. "Stupid," she muttered.

Pietro regretted what he had done and was trying to figure out how to make up for it. But she just turned her back and kept on eating the crust of bread she had found in the bread-chest. So he took out his pocket penknife, opened it, and stabbed her in the thigh. Though Ghisola went pale, she managed not to lose control. Thinking he hadn't hurt her, and still very cross and humiliated, Pietro took the knife and started to rush at her again, but she kicked him and ran into her room, throwing down the bread as she did so. When the old woman heard the furniture bumping about, she stopped sweeping and came into the house to see what was wrong with Ghisola. She was crying in one of those steady wails that stops as soon as it starts.

Pietro was left alone in the kitchen. He was so frightened he was laughing nervously under his breath. Just as he began to creep up to see what was happening, Masa came out. "Why did you make her bleed?" she shouted angrily. "There's no reason for you to be so cruel. I won't stand for it. I'm going to tell the master."

"It wasn't my fault."

By now Masa was beside herself and all but clouted him over the head.

Pietro, by this time, had come to believe he was telling the truth, even swearing to it with certain oaths he was delighted to have a chance to use since they had impressed him deeply ever since he learned them.

But Domenico and Anna made him apologize, beating him on the hands in the presence of Masa and Ghisola. Though the punishment itself felt good, almost, Pietro was mortified for a while—as though his games were bringing him close to some awful disaster. He began to be so superstitious and was so certain that sooner or later something terrible was going to happen that he stopped going out to play. He had had a premonition of this two years earlier when a stone he threw had hit another boy who he didn't know was hiding behind a hedge. So now his conversations with Ghisola began to be more serious, almost as if they had some new, hidden meaning.

When he met her alone in the fields a few months later, at first he walked away. But then he came back and managed to screw up enough courage to ask, "Did I hurt you a lot?"

His feet were sinking down into the freshly plowed earth and this made him feel awkward. But she gave him a smile.

"When?"

"When I stabbed you with the knife—but not on purpose."

That smile had already put him off balance and he had lost track of what he was going to say.

"Are you still thinking about that?"

Her attitude was completely unexpected and astonished him.

"You mean you've forgotten?" he asked.

"Right away."

What she was trying to say, it seemed, was, "Things like these are wicked. It isn't right even to think about them."

"But it must have hurt. If you want, you can do it to me, right now."

"I can?"

"I swear you can. You know that when I swear something, I keep my word. I hurt you, didn't I?"

And he showed her how to take the pen knife and stab him the same way he had stabbed her. She wanted to show him she was taking him seriously. "Whenever you're ready," she answered.

Now that she had agreed to do it, she really didn't want to any more.

"No one must know."

"I'll say I did it myself."

But when he took her hand to give her the knife, she broke free and grimaced in a way that made it clear she didn't believe him.

"Have I ever lied to you? My name's not Agostino!"

When he insisted, she looked so miserable that he left, hitting the tallest oat stalks with his hand and feeling confused and determined never to see her again. He was sorry he had met her and disgusted with himself too. "Maybe she said no because of her aunt and her grandmother," he thought.

Ghisola, quite to the contrary, was sure he hadn't meant it. She hated the master's son with the powerful hatred instinctive in all those who have to obey.

Besides, she wanted to believe he hadn't meant it—it gave her one more reason to dislike him. Whenever she saw him in the distance and he was too intimidated even to look at her, she would start to sing.

In school Pietro overflowed with nervous merriment that made him tease the students who sat near him. He got them to listen by calling them comic nicknames and insulting them if they paid no attention. When the others were quiet, he still couldn't understand the teacher, though the answers his friends gave rang in his ears like a strange admonition.

He was the biggest and slowest student in the last year of the elementary class and all the seminarians poked fun at him.

Sometimes, after trying to understand, he would force himself to follow everything the teacher said, enjoying the effort but regretting how the others kept thinking less and less of him. When he had been paying attention, his mind would be in a whirl afterwards and there was such a weight in his forehead that he wasn't able to study. Even though he hadn't done a thing all day, he would be exhausted. He would put down one book and pick up another and then put that down too—in the end not reading anything or even realizing that there were books in front of him.

At times like these he greatly enjoyed the restaurant's noise and bustle.

For all that, he was supposed to do his homework in front of the poorer customers. They all ate together at one long table from napkins in front of them. The cracks in this table held breadcrumbs that Pietro would pinch up and eat.

The customers of this sort were on good terms with Domenico and Anna and their stories always made Pietro laugh. "What are you doing in here wearing your eyes out?" they would say to him. "Go on outside and play."

But then Anna would get up from the dark corner behind the wooden screen with the peephole for watching the waiters and the wine cupboard. "Leave him alone!" she would say—and then she would laugh too.

In summer, when a little breeze was blowing, customers would be in their shirt-sleeves and you could see all the pipe and cigar smoke coming out the open window. But in the winter they passed around an earthenware hand-warmer.

They played lots of tricks on each other, stealing each other's wine or fruit. But when a customer cursed too much, Anna would blanch and look him in the eye. He would sit there with the words still on his lips while the others quietly changed the subject.

"No cursing. You have time for that outside. Out in the street!"

Then he would blush. "It wasn't me who got scolded yesterday, was it, mistress?"

Then they would all laugh and Anna would turn her thoughts to something else.

"How about a drink," someone would shout. "But not that watered stuff. Don't punish us for what happened!"

Anyone with wine still left in his glass would drain it and put the glass back on the table with the others. Calling for the flask, Anna would ask, "How much do you want?"

"A penny's worth."

"Two penny's worth for me."

Adamo held his glass up to the light.

"Looks like rain in the wine cellar again today!"

When a customer crossed through from one of the other rooms, they would all fall silent and watch him go by.

"There goes so-and-so."

Once in a while they would start to sing. But when that happened Domenico would charge from the kitchen waving a soup ladle. "Don't do it!" they would say, throwing up their hands. "We're going."

There were not many arguments and even when there were, friendships did not suffer for long. Usually they did not insult each other directly. Instead they took turns, explaining how they felt, looking at the others as though they were telling a story, quietly at first, but then more and more vehemently until they were on their feet cursing and slamming their fists on the table.

"Shame on you!" someone would say, just as the two people arguing would start to touch fists. "Think who might be listening to us!"

By the time Anna had started to have enough, the string of curses would come to an end, cut off by a huge mouthful going down.

Adamo would tease Domenico whenever he put in an order, mincing like a spoiled woman as he wheedled and asked him to take special care. Then, looking him straight in the eye but concerned that in the kitchen they were making fun of him, he would turn away to wait. After tasting what they brought him a couple of times and finding it to his liking, he would breathe easier, clear his throat, and start to eat. His good humor restored, he would be the first to stuff a piece of apple peel down Giacomino's neck and wake him up. Though he was old, fat and squat, and had a moustache that was forever getting in his mouth, Adamo had moods that changed just like a child's. Apologizing for his earlier bad manners, he would hunch down and drum his fingers on the table cloth. He was always chewing on a cigar that he rolled around his mouth, wiping his cheeks calmly with the back of his hand. He had no compunctions about eavesdropping on a long conversation in the next room and then putting in a couple of words or a sigh as his own opinion on the matter. But if they saw fit to answer, he would pull even deeper on his cigar and slump back into his revery.

Even when he was eating, Giacomino would prop his head on his hand and tug at the hair at the nape of his neck.

Bibe sat with his eyes down and his chin on his fist at the table edge, happy just to listen and not see anyone. Without making a sound, he would tap on the floor, one foot at a time, beating in rhythm until someone grabbed his curls and jerked his head around.

"God! That hurts! What fun do you get out of that?"

"Are you sleepy, you animal?"

"I sure am."

Smiling drowsily, he would tell them why he couldn't sleep properly.

They always insisted on the same seats—Adamo in the corner where he could spit all he wanted, Giacomino under the window, Bibe, the youngest, out of harm's way on the couch ready to drop off to sleep as soon as they left him alone.

When they were done they would rebutton their pants, fasten their belts, spit, shove and cuff one another, tweak each other's moustaches, and then pay as they left, going up in turn to Anna's cubbyhole.

And Pino? Pino, the old teamster from Poggibonsi, was the poorest of all. "Is there any room left for me?" he would shout, trying to get them to laugh.

They all did make room for him, in fact—not out of politeness but because they were sure he had fleas. Although he knew this, he got this same treatment everywhere and never dared say anything but just grumbled a little without getting angry.

"Half a place is enough for me. I'm no gentleman. Oh my, how my bones do ache!"

One of his eyes refused to stay open, the eyelid fluttering just like an owl's. He would survey the room with his other eye, always starting at exactly the same point. Afterwards he would stare at his hands so that everyone would know he had washed them. He did this in a dilapidated old horse-bucket that was in the same shape as his wagon shafts with their multiple wrappings of wire and twine. What a lot of time he wasted getting it fixed and ready each morning!

Smiling foolishly, he rubbed his eyes with one finger; his mouth, gaping wide in that smile, seemed twice as large as usual.

"You're laughing, are you, you rapscallion! What did you steal today? He steals part of every load consigned to him and claims he's lost it in transit."

"Me? You poor fool! Maybe I used to, but not anymore."

When he talked he drawled in a way that seemed both sincere and malicious. "I've got two grown daughters at home," he added. "Real beauties, both of them, if I may say so. But there's nothing left of my wife but a bale of greasy rags you wouldn't even want to put your hand on. And I've got these two girls, poor things! What in the world am I supposed to do with them?"

His whole face glowed with a humble but determined kindness and—strange as it may seem—his cheeks beneath the stubble were as delicate as a woman's.

He never ordered anything himself but let Domenico pick something out from the previous day's left-overs lumped together as a single portion. After he did this Domenico would grab his hat brim and pretend he was going to punch him in the nose.

"See what I've got for you?"

"Right, it's fine—stale but not too smelly."

Adamo and Giacomino would throw pieces of bread or bits of fruit at him. Without even looking in their direction, he would take both hands and pull them over as though intending to hide them under his plate.

"Today I feel better."

He always greeted Anna with great respect, waiting politely for her to answer and careful not to sit down until she gave him permission. So when Anna forgot, she had to tell him, "Oh go on and sit down!"

"Ah, I can sit down? I thought it might be too much trouble for you today. I'm exhausted."

And there he would wait with folded hands.

Almost once a month he made Pietro tell him the stories of the two colored lithographs that hung on the wall. Pietro would climb on a bench so he didn't have to take them down, but Pino would say, "Bring them closer to me! If you only knew, little Pietro, how my eyes are smarting! Sometimes I'm worried I'm about to go blind."

One was "The Battle of Adua" and the other "The Forgers of Italian Unity." Afterwards he would pluck at his sleeve, saying, "Don't pay any attention to your father. Study. I know what I'm talking about!"

Though he didn't know why, Pietro would pat him.

In the winter, when Pino was cold and wet and had his collar turned up to the tips of his ears and his hat pulled down to his eyes, Pietro would peer wordlessly into the old man's face until Domenico took him by the scruff of the neck and yanked him around.

When he died, no one even knew.

Another year, the end of March, St. Joseph's Day.

From Poggio a' Meli you could hear the jumbled ringing of bells all muddled like a deep crescendo high in the sky. Pietro was caught up in a strange exhilaration like a good mood that was so poignant it hurt.

I just have to say something about those ineffable March turbulences that are almost always connected to some subtle voluptuousness and the desire for whatever is beautiful.

The ambiguous sunshine, the still concealed and soon forgotten bird twitterings, the radiant clouds that seem to have emerged prematurely! And the dry leaves lying on seeds that have sprouted beneath them so that death's pallor and life's pallor are mixed together! Different varieties of leaves lying on the grass waiting for new life—the pruned trees with their branches and clippings heaped below them on the ground waiting to be carried away forever! And the dead limbs lopped from the fruit trees where new shoots are still hesitating before they burst into bloom! The damp earth that clings to the edge of the spade so that the peasants have to clean it off with their thumbs, and the clods stuck tight to their wooden clogs! The mysterious, almost conjugal affection of all living beings bound in assistance one to another—and their hatred too! The mistletoe slashed from the maples by the pruning hook but that soon will sprout again! And the chestnut buds!

Domenico, the farm hands behind him, tromped into the fields to arrange for the next day's work.

Though Pietro had put on weight, he was still pale and puny; before long he would be fifteen. He wore a jacket with a sailor collar that had been made over for economy's sake from an old suit. He thought it was ridiculous and inappropriate for a boy his age.

Quickly, he slipped into Giacco's house. As usual, the old man clapped a hand on his shoulder.

"How fast you're growing! I bet you brought me something to smoke."

Pietro took him by the moustache and swung his face back and forth. Giacco was careful to turn his neck so it wouldn't hurt.

Laughing, the boy looked over at Masa. "Harder," she said.

"No, no. That's enough."

Slowly but determinedly, Giacco pushed him away.

"Not even one cigarette butt then?" he asked.

When Rebecca swept out the restaurant she saved the butts for Pietro to take to him.

"You can be certain the little master doesn't smoke," Masa added.

Laughing as though she had just pulled off a practical joke, she grimaced and bit her lip. The old man took a pipe from his pocket that had a stem no longer than the palm of his hand.

"Thank God I've still got what his mother gave me last week. Look here if I don't!"

He knocked the pipe on the edge of the table; a sort of burnt powder fell out. Gathering this up, he mixed it around and stuffed it back in the pipe. Then he took a burning twig out of the fireplace. Bluish smoke straggled from his mouth.

"Not too much tobacco today," he said, gazing at it.

Using the thumb with the missing nail where he had cut himself as a boy, he tamped the bit of ember into the bowl.

But Pietro could see the smoke in two ways. Something was in it, something that came from deep inside him and made him as woozy as if it were real. His mother at home was trying to take something out of a drawer! But they had all gone and left her alone! As she kept tugging, the drawer vanished into the wall. Her hands on his face were like a huge kiss. It was as though her hands themselves were kissing him.

His vacant look astonished Masa. "What are you thinking about?" she asked.

The old man started for the door. "I have to go see to the cows," he said. "Hand me the lead rope."

But Masa was worried to see the little master in such a state. "Where did you leave it?" she snapped.

"Go find it," said Giacco.

"You never know what you're doing. And your wife is supposed to be there ready to hand you whatever you want."

"Such chatter! Couldn't you just find me the lead rope without answering back? Wouldn't that be better?"

"I can chatter all I want. Just as much as you can."

Then she turned to Pietro. "Have you seen Ghisola today?" she asked. He still seemed worried about something and she wanted him to snap out of it.

"Isn't she here?" he said absently.

"She was going to go to Siena for mass," said Giacco like someone who wanted an argument.

"Good for her. There's never anyone at Poggio a' Meli," Masa retorted.

"I'm surprised you didn't run into her," she told Pietro.

Suddenly a thought seemed to come over the old couple and they gave each other a look that Pietro couldn't fathom.

"As long as it's God's will," Masa sighed.

"About what?" said Pietro. "Tell me."

"Where is she?" he went on, sharply curious. "Is she coming home soon?"

It was clear he was bewildered. You could see it in his blue eyes, those utterly truthful eyes that instantly let everyone know what he was thinking, eyes with lids that felt they were made from warm water.

The horse hitched to the buggy that was tethered to the iron ring in the carriage yard was leaning on one side resting. Toppa was devouring a filthy bread crust he held clenched in his paws as he gnawed it.

When he saw Ghisola Pietro lost control of himself.

She had grown up. Her black eyes were like the two olives that everyone knows are the best on the branch. Her lips were narrow and her figure trim.

He could feel the excitement running through him. She was walking slowly. Her head bounced when she walked and her black hair was slick with oil and combed in a way he had never seen.

She kept her face down and was stifling a smile, moving slower and slower as if she had a secret she couldn't decide to reveal. Since this hurt his feelings and he wanted to tease her or tell her something she wouldn't like, he jumped in front of her like he used to when they were kids.

How beautiful she had grown since he last saw her!

Seeing her red hair-ribbon, her shoes shiny with lard, and her nearly new gray dress, he sighed jealously.

But she was so angry it didn't even seem possible.

"Get out of here," she yelled. "Your father's around. Don't come any closer."

When he persisted, she gave a twirl and brushed past just out of his reach. Pietro was speechless and couldn't even look at her. Already he felt insulted and humiliated. Why was she acting like that? She had gone into the house by now, hesitating first with one foot on the steps. He was ready to go in too and talk to her there. He felt faint, overwhelmed by some incomprehensible feeling, yet determined to do what he wanted.

Little by little, however, he began to feel mollified and happy again, as if there were nothing to reproach her about. Simultaneously, an intense voluptuousness began to steal over him.

Ghisola came back out of the house. She had taken off the ribbon, changed her shoes, and put on a faded red apron. Quiet and serious, she lifted her eyes toward Pietro, then walked, hips rolling, into the fodder shed. She picked up the hay that her grandfather had cut for her, put it in the basket, and then stopped what she was doing to take a sliver out of her finger. He felt as if he were that hand. Her inexplicable silence embarrassed him so much that he couldn't talk but shoved her instead—just a little shove, though she frowned and pretended she had almost fallen.

"Next time I really will push you down," he said.

"Just try it."

When she wanted to, her voice turned sharp and harsh and she squawked like a chicken. He looked at her disdainfully, convinced that she was supposed to obey him.

People don't usually notice a loved one's tone of voice—or if they do they can't describe it.

"Go away," she said.

The feeling this gave him was like being under water and he couldn't keep his eyes open, though he did manage to answer. "Ghisola, a month ago you told me you loved me. Don't you remember? I do, and I love you," he blurted with a laugh that finished in a stammer.

Ghisola seemed to be hearing a joke. She loved to play at making things up and telling the truth afterwards.

"I know, I know," she answered.

Entranced by her pretty apron pocket, he couldn't say a word. Then, all at once, he grabbed her tiny handkerchief with the coarse border of blue wool.

"Give it back."

Frightened that he had done something foolish, he handed it back to her.

"Did you hurt your finger?"

Just being able to talk was an accomplishment for him.

"What do you care? You don't even have to work. You don't do anything," she answered insolently and disdainfully.

But he took her seriously. "If you want," he offered, "I'll help you do your work."

Teasing now, she pretended he didn't know how to help her and pushed him away, saying that he wasn't trying to help her but wanted to put his hands on her.

Just then Domenico came back from the fields.

Quickly Pietro picked up an olive branch and began to switch the shed door as if he wanted to kill the ants that were crawling in a line across it.

Ghisola bent over abruptly and picked up an armful of hay, turned toward the pile, and filled the rest of the basket. When she tried to sling it over her shoulder, she couldn't manage and the bones in her arms seemed about to break through at the elbows.

Stealthily, so that his father wouldn't see, Pietro helped her. When Ghisola crouched beneath him she kept her keen black eyes trained on Domenico—eyes whose lids were as sharp as the blades of certain grasses. But Pietro was blushing and trembling because she had squeezed his hand when she bent over. The tenderness was so strong he almost fainted.

"This is what these feelings ought to be like," he thought.

Domenico was checking to make sure that the horse was tightly cinched. "Get him unhitched and turn him around," he bellowed. "Then fold the blanket and put it back on the seat."

The animal refused to turn and the whippletree got caught in the shafts. Even the look in Toppa's eyes, although no more hostile than usual, was flustering Pietro.

"Pull him toward you!"

All the strength had gone out of his arms and he had to let go of the bridle. His fingers got tangled in the bit that was covered with foul green foam. He was doing the best he knew how, partly because he was sure that Ghisola had come back from the barn and must have been watching. But the trembling was getting stronger. At first the horse's hooves just grazed him, but then they came down right on top of him.

Domenico took the whip and shook it in Pietro's face.

"I know exactly what's wrong with you. And I know how to set you right too."

After wiping her clog against the wall to get the manure off it, Ghisola came over to help.

Whip still in hand, Domenico went to talk to Giacco. He had been standing listening, dangling his arms and holding his thumbs inside his hands where the veins bulged beneath the skin like long still worms in topsoil.

Pietro was afraid to look Ghisola in the face, though she kept her eyes on him wherever he went. His legs were buckling and he felt a strange lassitude that unnerved him and made him feel slightly sick. Ghisola was still helping. When they took the red blanket from where it had been spread on the horse, they touched fingers. And when they put it back on the seat, they banged their knuckles so hard it hurt, though both of them felt like laughing.

Domenico leaped into the buggy and glared at Pietro. "Come on!" he shouted. "What's that on your lower lip? Wipe it off."

"Nothing," he said, terrified.

He was worried that what he had said to Ghisola might have stuck there. But then he was embarrassed at his foolishness, his heart thumping as if trying to break out of his chest.

Giacco and the farmhands took off their hats and waved goodbye. Pietro had just enough time to signal to Ghisola with the corner of his mouth, but she was watching the master closely and quickly furrowed her eyebrows. So Pietro concentrated on the head of the horse that was already beginning to pull the buggy out of the yard and broke into a trot as they reached the road. The light of the sun, setting more red than pink on the other side of the Montagnola, hung in the Siena sky. But the lines and circles the cypresses formed on the hilltops made him sorry to leave such an immensity.

Domenico, driving, nodded silently at people's greetings. But whenever he saw a girl he knew, he would smile, slow down the horse, and push at the center of her apron with the point of his whip. Pietro blushed, half shut his eyes, and looked the other way.

To get his mind onto something else, he began to stare at the horse's legs, which beat different rhythms according to the tunes that raced through his head. Or he tried not to notice the special odor that came from his father's clothes.

By late April Pietro had become so negligent that the principal refused to keep him at school.

Domenico beat him with his belt until Anna was crying too. But the next day no one said anything more about it.

"It's the evil curses of people who hate us," Anna explained to Rebecca.

Though she prayed every day to some saint about it, she could never talk it over seriously with her husband.

"Not today," he always told her.

If she tugged at his jacket, he would jerk away. "You take care of him," he would say. "Don't you start in too . . ."

She didn't dare insist because she feared he would take it out on Pietro, punching him dizzy and then claiming he had lost his temper.

Nor could she discuss it at night since just as soon as she brought it up, he would ball up his fists, shouting, "Let me sleep. I've been working since morning and I'm tired. You go to sleep too . . ."

Or he would ask her a question. "Did you count the money that we took in today? It has to be counted before you can come to bed."

If she tried to retaliate by lying silent, he would snatch her head right up off the pillow.

"Answer me!"

She would resist and try to argue, but sleep would finally get the best of her.

Once, during an argument at the restaurant, Pietro jumped up and announced, "I'm going to study art!"

A notary's copyist, who had just finished his meal, gave an enormous guffaw.

Pietro was astonished at the man's calm, gentle eyes gazing indulgently at him; he studied the man for some time.

He was fat and had a shiny, purplish face covered with pimples.

He was wearing a light-colored suit with a gold watch chain and had blondish hair and a low forehead.

"Don't pay any attention to him," he told Domenico calmly and with great conviction. "Teach him your trade. You restaurant-keepers can name your own prices."

Everyone laughed because they could tell he was referring to his own unpaid bill.

A mild tickling spread across Pietro from his chin to his forehead. "What's it to you?" he exclaimed.

The man reached into a leather case, took out an amber cigar holder that had a gold ring on it. Into this he stuck half a cigar. "Run out and get me a box of matches," he ordered.

And he threw a penny on the table.

Pietro looked at his father. Everyone was staring, their eyes and faces burning into him. His heart thumped.

"Go on then," said Domenico.

He snatched up the money and dashed to the tobacco shop.

At this the copyist began to laugh so hard it made his face red. "Make him mind as much as you can," he added, coughing.

Though Anna disliked this horseplay, she refused to intervene for fear of driving customers away. Domenico, on the other hand, was delighted, increasingly convinced his decision had been the right one. "Just mind what I tell you," he would say to Pietro. "You don't need any more schooling. All you have to know are the multiplication tables. Schools should be abolished and everyone sent to work in the fields. The land is the greatest of God's gifts to us."

"That's just what you think," said Anna, displeased.

"How long did you go to school?" sneered Domenico.

All he needed now was a quarrel with his wife! She shook her head.

"We've made a fortune without even knowing how to sign our names."

The customers thought this over. "He's still young!" they added, trying to make Anna feel better. "You can't tell how it'll work out."

"But even when I'm sixty and he's in his twenties, I'll still be able to bash his head in."

"Certainly he won't grow up big and strong like you!"

In the morning, if there was time after chores, they would have breakfast separately, but at night they all ate together—Domenico at the head of the table, Pietro between him and Rebecca, the cook facing his boss, and the two waiters on the other side. The dishwasher sat sideways so his back wasn't to the others at a small table where they also kept the plates and cutlery. Anna would stay in her own chair and watch for customers.

The cook had gone to smoke in the doorway and was lounging with his head and shoulders against the wall. Rebecca was carrying in some plates while the dishwasher ran skipping like a boy to tell the stableman to hitch up the horse.

Domenico drank another glass of wine. Then he took out his false teeth and, keeping his hands under the table, wiped them furtively with a napkin.

Anna picked up a shirt she was mending.

After a while, Domenico took the napkin and knocked the crumbs off his trousers, had Rebecca brush him off and Tiburzi grease his shoes while he gave some additional orders. Then he crept up on tiptoe behind his son, who was humming to himself and drumming his fingers on the windowpane for accompaniment. "Let's go out in the country," he cried, slapping him on the the back of his neck.

The buggy had already been hitched and Pietro got into it without saying a word. By sunset they were at Poggio a' Meli.

When Ghisola came out from behind the shed, she saw him standing alone in the middle of the farmyard, his hands plunged deep in his pockets.

"What are you doing?" she asked him solemnly and reproachfully. "Why didn't you come before? There was a time you could hardly believe it was true. Though what do I care!"

"I already know what you are going to tell me," she continued.

"Sure she knows," he thought. "Other people know everything about me. And I don't know anything."

That inner life of his that was always taking control! How he wished it were later and he was silently savoring everything he had felt but left unsaid! This was why he felt inferior to everyone else. It was only in his imagination, especially when he had just waked up, that he could tell Ghisola what he wanted to tell her.

The scratching of his collar on his chin shamed him even more.

The way Ghisola stared it was as though she was laughing at him too. He wanted her to stop and began to kick at an olive tree. But when he looked up, there she was, a smile on her face, watching him more intently than ever—but all just in fun; he was sure of it now!

The sunset was over and a shudder passed through Pietro; he couldn't bear her smile and was trying to forget he had ever seen it. Head down, he stood still, thinking she should realize he didn't approve.

Ghisola was fixing her hair, holding up the pins so he could see how new they were and then pricking him on the hands with them before putting them back in her hair. But he didn't budge.

In the weeds you could see the grass blades bending and the insects hopping up and down on them.

"She must know what I want," thought Pietro as Ghisola was pricking him. "I have to tell her. I have to."

Despite the encouragement of her red stockings, he was speechless and shaking when he went up to her.

You could barely see in the olive grove where close to the ground it was already dark.

"What do you want? Answer from over there. Don't come any closer."

Ghisola could tell that he couldn't take his eyes off her stockings, but her skirt was too short for her to cover them.

"Don't you know what I want?"

A chaste and gentle expression had come over her face.

"Don't you? Answer me."

She blushed in a way that changed her expression.

"I know."

But when he wouldn't stop coming closer, she took her hard lean hands and pushed him away.

Pietro was so happy his legs were shaky. Ghisola's eyes never left him. All he could see were those eyes; the darkness and the field seemed tied to his movements.

"Leave me alone now! We'll talk later . . . I said later!"

He could feel the evening stripping the flesh from his bones, obliterating him.

"I love you," Ghisola murmured.

And she dashed away from the shed—for now the master, breathing hard and head bobbing over his huge shoes, was trudging toward the farmyard. Pietro stayed where he was, chipping at the corner of the building with a stone he had found in his pocket. Though he skinned his knuckles doing it, he didn't even notice.

Domenico glanced over and then started laughing with the farmhand Enrico, who had been walking behind him.

"Are you crazy or something? What are you doing there ruining that wall?"

"At least the little slut ran off in time," he said to his helper.

"They're both still children. As far as I can tell, they're still just playing."

Enrico took their side because he thought the master was pleased for Giacco and Masa. But Domenico seized the chance to overrule him.

"You keep your mouth shut," he answered. "I know more about this than you do."

Enrico was quick to agree. "They'll be starting in before long all right," he said, swallowing the way he always did after making a pronouncement.

Pietro was afraid of a scolding and had already put Ghisola out of his mind, though the attraction he felt for her was still powerful. He went over to where his father had taken the horse by the bridle and was leading it into the road.

"Get in."

He had his eyes averted and was trying to clean the dirt from his hands.

When the horse balked in front of the gate Domenico started to whip him across the knees. The animal reared and backed up and the buggy crashed into the wall.

"Hold still. You're going to learn a lesson. And if you don't . . ."

And he whipped him.

"If you won't learn what you're supposed to do either . . ."

And he whipped him again.

"I'll teach you. You'd better hold still."

By now he had the whip end in his hand and was hitting the horse on the nose with the handle. When the horse shook his head Pietro started to get down.

"You stay in your seat. If you get down, I'll whip you too."

The farmhands were looking on nervously, impatient for the master to leave and worried he might turn and start to yell at them, maybe even whip them too.

The horse stopped moving and stood calmly.

Domenico gave the whip to Pietro and then stood in front of the animal buttoning his jacket.

"Mind that I want to be obeyed! See how you've stopped now? I'll just take my time about getting back in."

And to test him, he unbuttoned and rebuttoned his jacket, stopping whenever the animal moved his head. Then, first tightening one of the reins, he climbed in, hesitating with one foot on the step and then putting both hands on the buggy and vaulting over in a single motion to the spot next to Pietro. "Slide over," he shouted.

Pietro was too embarrassed to move.

"Slide over, imbecile."

"Stick to my orders," he said, turning abruptly to the hands, "or else I'll fire the lot of you. Those fields are to be turned tomorrow."

"Yes sir."

"Don't you worry."

"As if we couldn't turn them in one day."

"Just so long as it doesn't rain."

At this last comment the master glared as if he were about to rush out at the person who had spoken. Then, in a voice like a chisel on rock, he added, "If it does rain, you can rebottle the wine. Giacco, you can open up the wine cellar. That's what you have the keys for."

"Yes sir. Whatever you say."

Finally he thought of the restaurant, glanced at his watch and saw he couldn't stay any longer, and so they left.

The brief sunset had been dense with rain clouds. Pietro kept his hands in his pockets, thinking that if he were alone he would whistle a tune. In the darkness the horse's legs all seemed to hit the ground at the same time. The more he drove, the more annoyed Domenico grew at having forgotten to tell the peasants to ready the holes for the olive trees. He worried that his orders weren't being respected and the work was not being done right. He hated not being able to work alongside them. His frenzy to catch them at something they shouldn't have been doing drove him to a fury.

He thought about going back and checking if anyone was still loafing in the carriage yard, gossiping about him behind his back for all he knew. Noticing the clouds, he felt the urge to whip them on their way too.

Pietro, meanwhile, was in the grip of a melancholy dream. The horse and buggy were being sucked backwards into an endless fissure that yawned in his soul.

All at once, the taste of his mouth thick on his tongue, he heaved a deep sigh and let his head droop so suddenly and involuntarily that it seemed he was going to fall from the buggy.

"What's wrong?" screamed Domenico.

He concluded he was just sleepy and wanted to punch him.

At Vico Alto the cypresses were slicing through the air. Porta Camollia had turned a reddish color and far away in the city you could see the streetlights lit.

The trees on the avenue above the railway embankment swayed soundlessly, their branches outlined against the limpid, purple mountains; the Osservanza Convent looked gentle.

High beyond the roofs of Via Camollia the tip of the Mangia tower was white, almost radiant in the sky, though the iron frame and the bell were darker.

When Anna had an attack of convulsions, she would spend the next day recovering in her chair in the restaurant. Her face would be white and Rebecca, keeping close, would unlace her corset. But since the cooks and waiters always had questions for her, she would open up her eyes, look around blankly, shudder all over, and then tell them what they needed to know. To keep her husband from further worry, she refused to go to bed. But it made her feel terrible when she realized that at such moments she was unable to keep track of Pietro.

Anna felt she was completely cut off from life and had never done anything to help her son. When she did feel good about their financial security, her memories of when they didn't have any money would ruin the feeling.

"It's impossible for us to be as happy as we want to," she would say.

And she would feel so bitter at the years of tedium in her life that she worried she no longer know how to behave decently. The thought of death was constantly before her, her faith in God no longer a consolation.

When she felt like this and tried to look over at Pietro, she would be so unhappy it frightened her.

Her nerves had been ruined by the convulsions, a condition that prolonged the indefinable sadness and desolation—for she usually recovered all by herself without anyone's assistance.

Of course she hoped she would get better—not because she believed the doctor, but because she had Pietro.

But she couldn't talk to him. She knew he was growing up and that she hadn't made him a part of her or told him any of the things that might have consoled her. Even when she forced him to stay with her, they were like two people who had nothing in common.

Pietro, who refused to be dominated by her, made sure she didn't find out how much he loved her. For her part, she would get needlessly upset at his escapades so that whenever she tried to keep closer track of him, Pietro would get uneasy. When she wasn't able to keep him under her thumb for a while, she would try harder afterwards to make him capitulate.

"You don't have any respect for your mother!"

Losing his patience, he would slip off without letting her finish.

Anna would cry and confide in Rebecca. "Why get so upset?" she would answer half smiling.

Rebecca used to be Pietro's nurse and she wanted to stay on his good side. She was happy, almost, when Anna talked this way. But Anna didn't understand. "It's not up to you to apologize for him," she would say.

"Me?"

And then Rebecca would be upset.

When Pietro would see her crying afterwards, he concluded that she was trying to get him in trouble; this made him want to behave even worse.

Anna was accustomed to giving Rebecca and Masa advice on how to bring up Ghisola. This was a patronizing kindness, however—designed to make Ghisola more dependent as well. Though she did do some nice things for her, such as telling Masa not to give her so much work to do, and remembering at New Year's to give her a new dress that she had bought from a peddler who stopped his cart at the restaurant door.

Then Ghisola would bring her flowers—stolen most likely—and wish her a Happy New Year.

People from Domenico's village always ate at the restaurant when they came to Siena and would bring him news and greetings from his relatives, sometimes even a kerchief filled with fruit.

One of these men had a son, Antonio, who he wanted to learn the building trade—something impossible in Civitella. He asked Domenico to recommend him to a good foreman. On Sundays and holidays Domenico took to inviting the boy over to play with Pietro. So the two of them, since they were about the same age, were forced, even though they didn't really get along together, to become friends. In this way, Agostino, who couldn't stand Antonio, was displaced.

Frequently, when the two boys went for a walk, they did as the restaurant-keeper suggested and went to Poggio a' Meli. After a few months Antonio began to brag that he had been alone with Ghisola. Although his story was true, at first Pietro thought he was lying and felt stung and disappointed. It wasn't right for a friend to lie. What had he been talking about with Ghisola? And why had he talked to her in the first place without telling him?

How humiliating it was when nobody respected his feelings and his entire soul was broken into pieces.

Other people could treat him any way they wanted while he just stood there and felt his throat go tight with frustration, as he turned red and felt confused and abandoned. Nothing suited him. The streets wore him down, the sun shone too hot, his clothes didn't fit, his hands were too big. He was so exhausted from trying to think about something else and convince himself it wasn't so that he got all mixed up, his ears began to ring, and he was afraid he was about to keel over.

Then, with a jolt so strong it was almost sickening, he realized that with his face it was impossible to conceal his stubborn, forthright loyalty. The thought distressed him so much that he almost considered changing his way of living.

One Sunday he went to Poggio a' Meli with Antonio, vowing he would show Ghisola what a liar he was. But it embarrassed him to admit how concerned he was and he could sense his inferiority compared to his friend, who on this occasion even seemed taller than usual.

On the way they had already had one argument which ended with punches in the back. Although he was all ready to stop and burst into tears, he was appalled to discover that the other boy was enjoying himself.

Antonio could easily see that Pietro was upset.

"You'll find out if it's true!" he yelled.

"I went to see her the other day too," his friend responded at Pietro's silence. "She promised to be my girl and not yours."

Then, interrupting himself, he threw him a punch that Pietro brushed off with his hand.

Antonio was increasingly confident. "You won't even get close to her," he kept on repeating.

"Neither will you."

"I'll do what I want."

Making believe he was angry, he pushed up against him, white saliva dripping from his mouth. Even when he wasn't talking, you could see every one of his upper teeth, all healthy enough but as crooked as if he had just plunked them into his jaw. His nose too was bent over on one side.

"I'll be mad at you," said Pietro, trying his best to dissuade him.

"What do I care? Do what you want. I'm a friend of your father's and can come out here whenever I want. In fact, your father would rather have me than you at the farm."

Pietro felt defeated—what he had said was absolutely true!

After they walked a bit more, Antonio took his arm and peered into his face. "Aren't you going to say anything?" he sneered.

Then he spat on the grass, wiping off his mouth afterwards with the back of his hand.

"I'm going back," said Pietro.

"I'm not. I'm going to see her. Go on if you want."

"You come back with me."

But since he didn't want Antonio to see her either, when he kept going Pietro had to do the same.

When they arrived in the farmyard Ghisola was coming out of the house. She was on her way to the fields to call her grandfather and was just passing a lovely cherry tree at the beginning of a grape row.

Antonio wanted to show how much better he was than Pietro and quickly jumped into her way. But Ghisola giggled more at Pietro and made it clear that he was the reason she had stopped for them.

When Antonio went to get some cherries and left them alone, Pietro asked, "Is it true that you're in love with me and no one else? Tell me. If it's not true . . ."

"Only you . . ." she said softly. "Though that's not what Antonio wants."

But then his confidence vanished and all he could do was stare at his friend's back.

Ghisola could see what he was doing. "Don't you believe me?" she asked him, shaking her head. She spoke so calmly he felt better immediately.

"Don't let him know. Why did you bring him with you anyway?"

He could see she was disappointed and seemed to be reproaching him for not having come to visit her by himself.

She was so beautiful he forgot all about what Antonio said.

Antonio, meanwhile, came back, clearly with some plan in mind. He had eaten all the cherries in one gulp and had a finger crammed in his mouth trying to pry loose the pits which he then spat as far as he could. Trembling, Pietro snatched a bunch of cherries from between his fingers.

"Why are you stealing them from me?" Antonio burst out. "Go on and give them to Ghisola, why don't you?"

Pietro hadn't wanted him to say that and didn't know how to answer, so he just stood there holding the cherries. But Ghisola came to the rescue.

"I'll get my own," she said.

How sweet and intelligent she seemed!

But Antonio didn't give up.

"I'll bend a branch down for you if you can't reach them."

Pietro could see that he never missed an opportunity to do something nice for her, but Ghisola noticed this too.

"Don't bother," she said, smiling.

But she said it so rudely Pietro was startled.

"Why didn't I think of that?" he thought. "Now it's too late. And how pleased she would been if I had said it first."

The three of them stood quietly in a circle looking at each other. For an instant all their ill will vanished and they seemed good friends, though they knew they were involved in something unsaid too.

Ghisola seemed happier now; she pushed back her hair and tugged at her apron string as if she wanted one of them to untie it. Since he didn't know what to say next, Pietro assumed she was thinking about leaving.

The trunk of the cherry tree was a reddish black color and had deep gashes like axe wounds that were filled with hard, glistening resin. Over it swarmed a column of ants while another column marched in the other direction—ants Pietro could feel crawling on him. Close by on the crumpled grass lay a puddle of hardened copper sulfate. A fig tree with smooth, pinkish white bark and leafless branches that had tangled together in growing was leaning over a strawberry patch. You could hear the toads in the pruned red willows down in the bottoms. All the shadows seemed to have disappeared and the mist from the plowed fields was rising low in the trees.

Antonio could tell that Pietro was thinking about something and he gave him a shove. Trying hard to keep his balance, Pietro stumbled toward Ghisola. But because he was afraid Antonio might take it into his head to punch him right there in front of her, he said nothing. A strange smell that excited him very much seemed to be coming off her. Could it be that she had almost thrown open her arms to him? The thought drove him wild. What if she had?

"What can you possibly see in him?" Antonio said to Ghisola. "Can't you see how ugly he is?"

She had to deny this, if only out of respect. But she did so in a way that wouldn't offend Antonio either.

"What's it to you?" she said defensively.

At that moment Pietro was almost certain he was no longer alone; but even though Antonio didn't know what else to say, he couldn't look her in the eye. When he finally did look at her, she smiled back sweetly and ingenuously. Antonio didn't know what to do to keep them apart. "I'm going back to Siena," he announced as cruelly as he could.

"Let him go," Ghisola whispered softly, though loud enough for Antonio to hear.

When he heard this Antonio marched away, turning around furiously afterwards to ask, "Aren't you coming?"

Ghisola said nothing and gave no indication what her silence might mean. It was clear she wondered what Pietro would do. "I have to go," he choked. "My father . . ."

Her whole face turned hard and she began to look toward Antonio, who was standing a few steps away.

"Don't say anything to him!" Pietro begged.

"Go on and go then," she answered, head down.

But Pietro was certain that she loved him. When he caught up with Antonio, he took him by the arm and they started to snicker.

"Why did we come to Poggio a' Meli anyway?" Antonio asked innocently, hoping that this would make Pietro stop thinking about Ghisola. "We didn't have any fun."

A locust sang in an olive tree. The millet swayed, first in slow waves, then more quickly. From time to time a stalk would seem to shudder and its light-colored flowers would burst into bloom.

Antonio reached in his pocket and took out a knife that had a bone handle carved like a fish; he slipped the blade beneath the husk on a length of cane he had picked up. Slashing at the knots with blows that sounded just like his laughter, he proceeded to trim the cane.

Although Antonio was pretending to be absorbed in what he was doing, Pietro didn't want him to copy him and didn't turn around to see if he could see Ghisola. Antonio, in fact, was watching him closely—even though he knew he didn't need to.

Back at Porta Camollia they cleaned their shoes with their handkerchiefs, mopped the sweat from their faces, and straightened their hats, helping each other with the creases.

Before going into the restaurant they promised that neither one of them would have anything more to do with Ghisola.

Ghisola had continued walking into the fields, giddy with a joy that filled her whole being. The motion her legs made under her skirt, a skirt so light she could hardly feel it, increased the sensation.

Antonio was perfectly capable of telling the master everything and she didn't trust him at all. Pietro meant nothing to her while Agostino was the worst of the lot.

Just then, Agostino arrived. He had been running through the grape rows, leaping over the stands of young wheat that grew between them, and he rushed over to her the way he did when he was out with a stick smashing pumpkins. He was in shirtsleeves, his wrists round and solid and the veins taut in the firm flesh. He had no hat on and his glittering ice-green eyes seemed to have no eyelids.

When he pushed up against her and knocked her down, she started to cry.

"Did that hurt?" he asked rudely.

"Not in the slightest."

Leaping up, she grabbed him around the waist and tried to do the same thing to him. But Agostino pinned her arms down. Smiling through her tears, she dug in her heels and tried to break free. But Agostino knew how strong he was. "I can do whatever I want with you!" he screamed in her ear. "I'm not going to fall and you know it!"

So she bit him on the arm. But Agostino pushed her head back with his arm until she had to let go. "Now what are you going to try?" he demanded angrily.

"What if I am weaker," answered Ghisola, spitting. "Are you proud of it? How salty your skin tastes!"

"When did you last see Pietro?" he asked threateningly, looking her straight in the eye.

She stuck out her tongue.

"He doesn't come around here any more."

From the house, Agostino had recognized Pietro by his clothes and had come out to talk to him. But he pretended to believe what she said.

"Is that so?"

"That's so."

"Did you think I was going to come and eat cherries with him?"

Again he lunged at her, trying to trample on the toes of her shoes where all the seams had come loose.

"Why didn't you tell me the truth? You can lie all you want to other people, but don't do it to me."

He was still trying to knock her over. Instead they both fell, butting their foreheads as they went down. Although he was ready for a real fight, just then he heard the jingling of his mule's harness bells.

"That's my brother coming back."

Kneeling first so he could hear better, he got up the rest of the way and rushed off yelling, "If he's been running her too hard. . . If he's been running her too hard! He has no idea how to handle her."

A pointed lock of sweaty hair was hitting him in the eyes and with his ears so tight to his head and his skull all round in the back he looked just like a soccer ball.

Ghisola lay still at first, sorry now that she had ended up on the ground like that. But then she sprang to her feet and began to brush herself off, inspecting the heels of her hands the way she did after a nap in the fodder field.

When she was cutting fodder and had to straighten her clothes—her shirt especially, which was always coming unbuttoned—she would stick the sickle into a tree trunk. After clenching her hairpins tight in her teeth, she would put them back one by one into her oil-slick hair. When she touched it with her finger, the point of the sickle would be all wet from the bruised wood as if from saliva. Then she would stand up and, in fits and starts, begin to sing. After that she would spit on her hands and bend back to her job.

Sometimes she wanted to cover her face and just lie there invisible to everyone except the sky. Or she would decide to stop eating and die without even knowing what happened.

Sometimes she had urges to scream—terrifying urges.

Though Anna didn't have very much time for the farm, when she did have time and there was nothing to do in the house she would have Ghisola fill some jugs, take the watering can, and water the lemon trees. In the evening Giacco would hoe the weeds that grew round the house and toss them to the rabbits or the chickens.

Anna would go all the way down to the vegetable garden and have one of the women pick her some lettuce and cabbage.

She would have liked a flower garden, in part because near Poggio a' Meli there was one she often admired and would like to have owned. But she had to be content with her geraniums and carnations—that is, whenever she got some starts from someone. She didn't dare have too many either, for if she did Domenico would certainly want to know whether she was in the country for her health or on vacation. Even so, just knowing that now she had more flowers than when she was a girl gave her a feeling of satisfaction.

As for the knick-knacks in the living room in the city house, she had almost been forced to purchase them. Every time the Jewish secondhand dealer had a restaurant bill to settle, he would bring a lot of old things for her to see. Despite her protests, he would leave some behind on the counter. When he came back a week or so later, Domenico and Anna would argue for thirty minutes whether or not he could settle up like this again. The secondhand man would promise cash on the line from then on. Then, since the insults and shouting had made them hoarse, they would all have a glass of wine.

Anna, however, liked this arrangement and this is how the glass paintings of *The Five Parts of the World*, the vases of yellow alabaster, and the genuine porcelain jars all came into her house.

By now the living room was chock-full. One entire wall was covered with photographs of almost everyone they knew while nearby a pair of plaster Roman peasants stood smiling on a walnut-stained table. In the center of the room on a smaller table there was a set of light blue crystal that was nearly complete. Ranged around it were five little brass lamps with tasseled handles that they kept for Good Friday when they would send them over with a flask of oil for the Feast of the Sepolcri.

At least once a month she would clean the floor with red ochre and when she did you had to wipe your shoes carefully before going in.

When she was in the country and people would bring flowers, she never kept them; she would take them instead to the Madonna at the convent at Poggio al Vento. When it was late and they had closed the church, she would put them in water—but on the hall table until the next morning.

She had an old red ivory-handled umbrella to keep the sun off, since otherwise she soon got a headache. But she was self-conscious about it and whenever she met the farmhands' wives she would close it up and stand under a tree instead. All the same, she liked to have it with her when she went to mass and sometimes would get Ghisola to carry it.

In church, she would take a pew not too far from the peasant women. They, in turn, knew enough to show her some respect and would make room without being asked.

She had a tailor-made black dress with yellow silk trim around the collar and a lace bodice that went half way down her sleeves and was attached at the shoulders and waist. On the trim she wore a gold chain. But in the restaurant she wore a red dress with blue and white polka dots.

She would often tell Ghisola she should learn how to write, at least a little. Since she couldn't trust Pietro to give her lessons without making fun of her, when she was feeling well she spent a few hours a day with her herself. Ghisola even got some wild mulberries and made ink from them. But she never got further than the first letters.

In truth, however, Ghisola would have liked to learn. It impressed her to think that Pietro went to school. She wished that at least she knew how to read. A lot of her girlfriends at neighboring farms even had their own prayerbooks—the kind the Capuchins gave away for First Communion. On Sunday mornings when she went to Siena to the Piazza del Campo she wanted to buy the penny broadsheets with their tales of miracles and illustrations of the Madonna with a big crown behind her head. The songs were wonderful and always had pictures too, just before the words. She would stop and listen with the others whenever she saw Cicciosodo singing these songs and playing his guitar. He was the storyteller who sat on a tall stool and could move his stovepipe hat by tightening the skin on his forehead. There were monkeys too that picked out the numbers for *The Wheel of Fortune* and a man who sold colored candies in paper tubes with scissored fringes.

By the time she got back to Poggio a' Meli, she knew the tune of her favorite song by heart, though she could never remember the words. Sometimes, when she bought the broadsheet anyhow, keeping it folded in her pocket so that Masa wouldn't see, she would go out in the fields and get a girlfriend to read it to her. Some parts of the songs would be so pretty they would make her laugh or cry.

Pietro needed something to keep him occupied. He had a talent for drawing and Anna, along with certain customers, thought it was worth developing. So she sent him to art school.

One morning when he was home copying an ugly printed portrait Pietro suddenly asked himself why Ghisola made him feel so strange.

Experimenting, he lengthened, then shortened the neck of the portrait he was working on. No matter how hard he tried, the drawing came out insipid and wrong.

He was amazed that he couldn't get it right and pursed his lips til they almost touched his nose.

His old schoolbooks lay dirty and with broken backs under his feet. He felt uncomfortable and couldn't concentrate when he touched them. The drawing was getting on his nerves too.

A familiar giddiness that prevented him from doing anything flooded his brain like icy spring water. Just existing seemed strange and he became so frightened that he tried not to think about it, staring so long at his upturned hands that finally he couldn't see them any more.

At this he felt a twinge behind his left shoulder blade and his whole being seemed concentrated in that spot.

After a time he realized that the desk where he was working was too low for him and had made him feel even groggier.

He got up. The pencil fell and broke apart. He picked up the pieces with almost superstitious disappointment—"Why had it fallen?"

Hurt and discouraged, he examined the portrait and then the copy—as if the doubt and hesitation that were forever bothering him had reached a kind of peak.

Meanwhile, a ray of sunshine, a beam loaded with drowsiness, had taken over the entire piece of paper. "It's over," Pietro thought. "I can't go on any longer."

"What are you doing sitting there doing nothing?" asked Rebecca, who had just finished sweeping out the bedrooms and was passing by.

He jumped after her and locked his crossed hands in front of her face. Rebecca laughed through her closed lips until his fingers were all covered with spit. He rocked her head back and forth, then leaped away and went into the other room.

That same morning Ghisola refused to get up. Masa was furious. "What's wrong with you, lazy bones?" she asked.

When Ghisola didn't reply the old woman went grumbling into the kitchen to have her breakfast. After a little, she opened the door again and stuck her head in. "Why don't you answer me?" she repeated. "Are you going to just lie there and make faces all morning?"

Ghisola muttered something and hunched further down under the covers, her face turned to the wall.

Masa was holding a bowl of half-eaten cold soup in her hand. She could not stay angry for long and was eager to make peace. "I saw you laughing," she said.

Ghisola was dead tired—so exhausted that the sensation, as sometimes happens, was almost a moral one.

But Masa, exasperated, kept after her. "I'm not going to waste any more breath on you. I'm not accomplishing anything here with you."

"Don't then! Can't I sleep? I don't feel like working. Don't I have to go back to Radda anyway? What are you doing standing there stiff as a board?"

She felt as though she hadn't slept a wink and it astonished her that Masa kept on talking. "You don't have to get insolent with me just because the master doesn't want you here any more."

Masa pretended she was going to hit her in the face with the spoon; instead, she just licked it on both sides. Deep down, she sympathized and was sorry they had to part. She went back into the kitchen.

Talking with Masa had made Ghisola feel better and she decided to get up. Dressed in her nightgown, she took some artificial flowers and pieces of wire that had had grapes on them the year before and made them into a garland. She hid this in her bureau next to the colored paper bits, containers of perfumed soap, and the pile of ribbons and strips of cloth she liked to display on her windowsill where the pair of pigeons would beat on the glass with their beaks, begging for the corn or breadcrumbs she kept in her apron pocket.

She refused to eat, however, even though Masa had already cut her a piece of bread.

"What do you live on? Other times you stuff yourself silly."

Throwing open the cover of the bread-chest, the young woman thrust her head inside. She could smell the sour odor of yeast coming off the loaf where Masa had cut a cross in the crust with the back of a knife.

Then, her mind still fixed on her ribbons and fragrant boxes and singing at the top of her lungs, out she went to the fields.

She did most of the cutting where the grass was thickest. Where it was short and thin she could finish quickly with a single slash of the sickle. From time to time she wiped her wet hands on her skirt. The young shoots of heavy fodder corn drove her almost wild with joy and she kept the nicest stalks on top so that she could give them to the heifers herself. They would gobble them greedily, licking her hands and wrists afterwards, shaking their heads and rattling the chains that hung from their horns.

All that chewing in the quiet of the barn! And the way they drank from the overflowing troughs, the odd sucking sounds and the movements their tongues made, breathing through their nostrils with their necks extended so far that their mouths fell open as they pushed sideways at the trough.

But this time she burst into tears, slammed the door with all her might, and ran back to her grandmother.

Ghisola was no longer well behaved. She had turned stubborn, developed unsuitable ambitions, and insisted on having her own way.

After dinner on Sundays she would disappear from the house until dark. Her grandmother would search the nearby farms for her— but she was out on the streets of Siena listening to the suggestive compliments and indecent proposals people made her. Men who knew who she was would follow after her and try to make her stop and talk. She would smile, flattered and a little bewildered at this attention from people who weren't peasants but well-dressed city workers. But when she got to Porta Camollia she had to hurry past the customs guards who would come out and try to block her path.

If she was wearing a flower she had to stay away from the walls because there were plenty of men standing in doorways ready to reach out and grab at it.

To avoid a scolding when she got home, she would climb up on the chicken-coop mountings and go in through the bedroom window. Undressing in the dark, she would go to bed without any supper though when she heard the brass spoons ringing against the soup bowl where Giacco and Masa were eating she would be furious. Giacco would look at Masa every time the spoons knocked together.

In time her grandmother would realize she was back and, thinking she wasn't feeling well, would sneak her a piece of bread. But before handing it over, she would first give her a rap on the head with it.

Face to the wall, Ghisola would munch at the bread, amazed afterwards to find it soaked with her tears. Only a moment before she had felt like laughing. Was this what her life was going to be like?

When she heard her grandparents come in she would shut her eyes so that they would think she was sleeping and she wouldn't have to look at them.

Her last day at Poggio a' Meli she was chewing an old hairpin and just about to fall asleep when she seemed to be falling from a great height and bumping to a landing on the roof of her house at Radda. She began to toss and moan.

"Be quiet!" said her grandfather from the other bed. "Do you think we like to hear stuff like that?"

She didn't want to get a scolding. But then it occurred to her, and she said out loud, it seemed, "It doesn't matter to them any more. Just as long as I don't snore."

But the odor of her unwashed sheets was starting to bother her and she wrapped them around her neck so as not to smell them.

Her hair was undone and looked like a scythe where it came to a point on top of her pillow.

She seemed to be walking into her house. Her mother had a new dress and her two sisters had put on weight.

"What are you doing here?" demanded a voice.

"I don't know," she answered. "I didn't come by myself. Where's Daddy?"

"It's all your fault," the voice answered.

Her mother and sisters were listening, watching her so quietly it was horrible and she wanted to lunge at them and chase them into another room. But she couldn't lift her arms and her head was hitting an invisible wall. She could feel her heart and her stomach changing positions and the skin start to peel from her neck. Her mother's and sisters' faces had begun to terrify her.

"Say something!" she said.

They turned toward the door. Up the stairs came her father, two huge sacks on his back and blood dripping down his face: so much blood it could have filled a mill-race.

When she could feel the weight of the heavy sacks pressing down on her she started to scream.

Pietro was crazy about wild flowers, pale wild flowers with such faint fragrances you could hardly tell one from the other. But even the thought of garden flowers made him blush in confusion. He got into the habit of filling his pockets with them: red and white daisies, yellow dandelions, pale pink vetch, poppies, broom, violets, wild hedge roses, hawthorn, wild sweet peas. Then he would chew on them.

Ghisola had taught him how to make mulberry ink, how to suck the honey taste from those reddish flowers like wild lilies that grow under the ears of the wheat in the wheatfield, and how to tell when the red hedge berries are ready to eat. She did this so that when he saw her skipping over the furrows in the fields—and certainly not on her way to work, either—he wouldn't throw dirt lumps at her.

One morning, during breakfast, he discovered that Ghisola had gone back to Radda. Rebecca was telling Adamo about it. Though he didn't stop eating, he lifted up his face to hear better and then just sat there all day with his head hunched between his fists.

Rain was coursing down the window pane almost as if it were trying to flood the room. It was a gusty rain, the kind that smacks against walls as though trying to push them over and then suddenly turns clear and transparent and starts to come straight down, changes directions, and finally disappears until all that is left are occasional drops that strike your face like points of cold needles. The roads change color, catch their breath, and are flooded with sunlight that afterwards turns to shadow and then back to light. From behind the Montagnola clouds rush out as if from hiding and stream toward Siena; others slip behind Mount Amiata.

Roads that rush off in all directions, bump together, retreat, join up again a couple of times, and then come to a halt as if uncertain which way to go; steep, crooked, tiny, sunken squares robbed of space by the ancient buildings crowding on top of them.

Lines and circles of twisting houses so jumbled it seems each street is trying to go its own way; fragments of country peeping crookedly through the slit of an alley, or church steps, or a forgotten, deserted loggia.

In his fantasy Pietro thought that for punishment they were forcing Ghisola to walk alone in the rain. By the time he fell asleep he had been thinking about this for a long time.

He had already wasted a whole year at the art school and nothing had been resolved. They had to consider the advice of all the faithful customers as well as that of his father, though he didn't bother to think much about it and, when he did, would only get irritated. Anna was patient and kept bringing it up, even after the unfortunate experiment with the drawing, for she was sure that her son was intelligent. But fate prevented any further help from her.

One morning she decided to go with her son and seek advice from the local priest. She had already taken out her nicest dress and was trying to hurry so her husband wouldn't know. Suddenly, unable even to scream, she felt her heart being squeezed tighter and tighter. When she hit the ground she didn't even know it.

They found her on the floor next to the open wardrobe, face forward like an animal that has just had its skull kicked in. Her eyes were half open and still full of life, her expression only slightly contorted, almost as if what bothered her most about dying were its effects on other people—as though she were begging them sadly and carefully not to blame her for it.

Rebecca, who had gone in to fix her hair, was the first to find her. Quickly she uncapped her convulsion medicine, but Anna was no longer breathing.

"Mistress! Mistress!"

Trembling and terrified, she raced into the kitchen, pushed her head through the window opposite the restaurant entrance, and began to scream. A waiter heard her.

"The master. Tell him to come right away!"

The waiter, who thought it was an especially serious fit of convulsions, put down the rag he had been holding and went into the kitchen.

"Where's the boss?"

"He's not back yet; he's still out settling with the grocer."

"Go find him right away! The mistress doesn't feel well!"

It was the dishwasher who had heard him and he put down the knife he was using to clean some fish he had just taken from a basket and piled on the sink. Wiping his hands, he tucked his apron up into the drawstrings and left. But Domenico had gone off to make a purchase and it took him some time to locate him.

Once he found him, they came back running. Going up the stairs Domenico met his friend and longtime customer, the doctor, who was just coming down to wait for him.

"My dear Domenico . . . Just wait and listen a minute!"

The restaurant-keeper seized him by the shoulders.

"Domenico," said the doctor, taking his wrists and pushing his hands away, "this time . . . the poor woman!"

"Let me go," he bellowed. "It's convulsions."

But he could feel a chill come over him, waves of cold that began at his fingertips and swept all the way to the center of his head. At first he thought he was losing his mind, but his heavy breathing—

he whose breathing was always so regular—made it evident that his premonition had come to pass. How could he face it? How could he look at Anna dead? Did he really have to go in there?

When he did go into the room the walls were swaying and the doors flying open by themselves and he couldn't see anything. When he touched her face, which was already stiffening and growing cold, he shut his eyes, hurled himself on top of his wife, and began to weep.

His own sobs made him shudder.

Little by little he began to get a grip on his grief. All his tremendous violence seemed transformed into fear—Poggio a' Meli seemed borne far off into the distance, and nothing he could do would stop it. He could feel the restaurant doors slamming shut by themselves, never to be reopened. He was sure that Anna, because she hadn't been able to say anything, had suffered enormously. Everything was going to pieces inside him.

His grief was so enormous that everyone would have to pity him! How sorry he was he had never loved her enough!

Bit by bit, Anna had grown colder. Someone had closed her eyes and it was only now that the crowd around her began to find her unusual or unfamiliar.

"I wonder what she was trying to say!" said somebody, taking her sympathetically by the chin. "How she suffered! Poor woman! Such a good person!"

By the time Pietro saw her she had already been laid out on the bed and he didn't know what to think. Domenico spoke to him only when someone reminded him to—but without warmth and almost as though he wanted to avoid him, though at that moment it was more important than ever that he stay on with him in the restaurant. His bellowing was so loud they could hear him out in the street.

"She almost looks ready to get up from bed," said Rebecca.

Suddenly Domenico approached her again, stroked her hair, gestured desperately, and began to bawl even louder. Pietro, who felt nothing except a vague uneasiness, leaned on the pillow and tried to cry. He was wondering secretly if the others felt as little emotion as he did. When they took his father away and he couldn't see or hear him any longer, he felt indescribably better since he found his grief just as hateful as his rage.

"Your poor mother," said Rebecca. "She loved you so much."

But all this hardly mattered; in fact he resented what she had said and went off embarrassed to try to forget it.

The morning of the funeral he had forgotten everything when, suddenly, through the half-open door, he saw his father coming to get him. Though he had no reason to think so, he was terrified he was going to be beaten bloody.

"Get dressed," said Domenico. "In a little while they're going to take your poor mother away."

Pietro tried to obey. By now he was worried something awful was about to happen.

He got up and, getting dressed, began to mime the gestures of grief he had seen.

His behavior soon created a silent hilarity that was mingled with terror.

When she was ready to go into the coffin and they made him kiss her, a thought came to him. "Why don't I climb in there too? Put me in there."

An incredible sense of alarm took over. "You think she's dead? You're all just acting. It's all an act. I knew you were going to do something to hurt me, but I haven't done anything to deserve this."

Overcome by desperation, he began to whimper. Why didn't they tell him earlier that she was dead?

Though he hung back with the people preparing the body, he refused to touch even the hem of her dress. He was amazed that the others, for all their tears and seemingly endless gestures of affection, were working away as if there were nothing unusual. Propping her head on a special monogrammed pillow, they shoved her feet together and replaced a flower in her hair from where it had fallen between the coffin and her shoulder.

He didn't want anybody to be there. All those hands scurrying over her bothered him. Those hands, those hands!

"Get her out of here right now," he wanted to shout. "Why don't you get her out of here? I don't want her at home any more." It astonished him that his father had kept his composure and even seemed calmed by the attention.

He decided to follow the funeral in a closed carriage whose worn blue silk curtains he nervously pulled down so that no one could see him. Domenico, however, had made up his mind to go on foot, partly to save money no doubt. Pietro was fascinated by the people who stopped in the middle of the street or even in front of their doorways to watch them go by. He noticed they stood up and craned their necks for a better view.

Anna's death was a great blow for Domenico. His staff no longer worked as they used to. His embarrassment made him so uncontrollable that he was more irritable than ever and frequently shouted for no reason at all. He began to be preoccupied with saving money and he had to abandon several projects for the farm and the restaurant. He was forced to work harder now too and disliked getting so worn out. As for his son, there was no way he could keep an eye on him the way he should have. He left him almost entirely to his own devices, although when he did think about him he would often treat him so roughly and with such undue rudeness that even Rebecca would come to Pietro's defense. When this happened, he would let up, but only to act even worse at the very next opportunity, almost as if he had to get even.

Anna died the second week in January. Sunday mornings, before the sun was up, the restaurant-keeper would take two bunches of flowers out to her grave. He would have preferred to take one and have Pietro take the other, but Pietro refused to obey.

"Why are you doing this to me?" Pietro would say, humiliated and knees buckling under the blows. "You don't have to kick me."

What if somebody recognized him?

The streets would be dark and damp and the sky just beginning to fill with those huge luminescences that signal that the dawn is still far away.

There would usually be only a few people going by and you could hear them talking distinctly, their voices just as clear as their hobnailed shoes on the cobblestones. One of them, maybe a porter on his way to the trains, would stop and cup both hands over a match to light his pipe.

About half way to the cemetery Domenico would stop at a cafe. The girl who worked there wore a dress cut so low Pietro was afraid it was going to fall off.

She laughed and joked with the customers, her firm, fat, powdered cheeks puffing out until she had to half-shut her eyes, serving up her smile the same way she did the gold-filigreed porcelain cups.

Pietro never wanted to go inside and Domenico would have to come back and drag him in.

The girl would flirt with Domenico while Pietro stood with his head down, embarrassed for her and the way she was acting, the same way he was embarrassed by the huge mirrors that covered the cafe walls. He couldn't even drink his coffee and would scorch his mouth and fingers.

Slipping out again before his father had time to finish, he would peer through the steam-covered windows with the long crooked drips as his father laughed and joked with the girl.

Once the sky cleared, the light would fall with a special clarity on the tower of Palazzo Pubblico and the air would fill with swallows. They darted past, giving off shrieks as long as their swoops. Piazza del Campo would turn all pink except for a few strips of green grass and the small white pillars in the fountain.

"Next Sunday I'm going to walk in without being told."

But he grew more timid each week and was made almost sick; just thinking about it he could feel a cold sweat on his forehead. Fists in his pockets where his fingers were clenched to the linings, he would stand unable to move.

Domenico walked slowly too, for that matter. When he had a cold he would stop, take out his handkerchief, and blow his nose.

It made Pietro feel even worse when they went up Via della Città and into Via di Stalloreggi.

When they got to the cemetery Domenico would stop and gossip with Braciola, the white-moustached gravedigger who was the same color as the dirt he turned and so fat he looked stuffed with worms. He would put the bouquets in two tall, porcelain vases that always had the same meager drops of brackish water in them. "How fast it expands!" he would exclaim, looking around. "The graves only came up to here when your mother died."

His father stood quietly for a moment. "Has the widow been here yet this morning?" he asked.

"Maybe she got here before we did," said Pietro. "Come on, let's go. There's no point waiting for her."

"It's early. Why don't you want to wait? She brings flowers every morning."

He resented his son's lack of interest—interest in her, the only other person who came to the cemetery the same time they did!

But the widow thought her loyal devotion was being compromised. Why did Domenico Rosi have to behave the way she did, when the whole city knew that he hadn't worshipped his wife nearly as much as he was trying to make out?

Whenever he said hello to her, she would give him a suspicious look and answer in confusion. And then there was the impression that the boy made—not even minding the graves and with his hands always in his pockets and a sleepy or sullen expression on his face!

"I'm going back," Pietro broke out.

Their clashes were becoming more and more serious. "Go on then," Domenico said near the end of winter.

"What do I care about her?" said Pietro, reddening.

The dew had turned the dirt on the fresh graves into sticky mud. Some birds flew across in front of them, heeling over on one wing as they went. The mountains between the cypresses looked like long strips of wet paint.

The tombstones were covered with gray snails. The Cathedral kept turning a brighter and brighter white; as he watched it, Pietro realized how furious he was.

At the gate they met the widow and Domenico said hello. Answering, she didn't even turn around, though she did keep one eye on Pietro. Domenico halted. "She's on her way to her husband's grave," he repeated, just as he always did.

Everybody knew who she was, though by sight only, and Domenico knew just as little as the rest. After she got back from the cemetery, where she always prayed for at least half an hour, she would do her shopping and then disappear until the next morning.

She was short and fat and her breasts, which only her swollen belly kept up, wobbled when she walked. Her hat was too small; she kept it on with a piece of black elastic threaded over her ears and under her chin. At every step she took, its worn, greenish feather flapped as if something were hitting it. Her thin hair was pulled tight by a hair pin; through it you could see the greasy back of her neck as red as goose skin. No one could remember ever seeing her dress any other way—and not just because she was short of money, either.

"What are you thinking about?" Domenico asked his son who had been following her with his eyes.

"Me? Nothing," said Pietro, smiling.

"Then why are you standing there looking down like that?"

"I didn't know I was!"

"You look terrible—not the way I want you to appear in public at all. And why do you want to go back to school, anyway? Didn't you get yourself sent home?"

Domenico was resentful when they talked about school and always brought it up when he thought he could make something of it.

Although he felt faint, the boy said nothing. His father never failed to throw that into his face, exploiting the subject for all it was worth.

"You could help out more in the restaurant," Domenico continued, seeing how confused and humiliated he was. "Then, in a year or so, you could get married."

Now that the restaurant was without a woman, Domenico would have been glad to marry him off. As if to make sure it wasn't too early, even if he was only sixteen, he checked his build and appearance frequently.

"I . . . I'm not going to get married."

"Well, think it over carefully. If you don't, I'll have to get re-married myself. What would you think about that?"

Though he was determined not to be badgered out of going back to school, Pietro hesitated. "To whom?" he asked.

His father was trying to find out how he really felt and just stared at him. "I'll let you know soon enough," he answered.

Pietro reacted as though it didn't concern him. "People say that that lady . . ." he went on, "the one with the two daughters . . . who came again to eat at the restaurant the night before last."

But this was just gossip and nothing more. "It would be a whole lot better if you married one of the daughters," Domenico answered.

"Me?"

This too seemed completely foreign to him, even though the idea excited him a little; he blushed again.

"I'll tell you the one I'd pick out for you."

"I know which one," he laughed. "The younger one."

But by now Domenico had fallen silent, thinking that when he had talked to his farmhands the previous night he had forgotten to tell them to put the cows to the bull for freshening.

"Why discuss this if you won't even answer?" Pietro managed to ask.

"You're not to butt into my affairs," Domenico shouted angrily. "Wouldn't I feed your wife too? Now stop it! Look—you were supposed to go to Poggio a' Meli!"

And, as invariably happened on occasions like this, he took a tarnished silver crown from where he kept it with some English gold pieces in his vest pocket. Crossing himself first with such a broad gesture he almost hit his forehead, he began to deliver his usual speech.

"See this? I keep it with me always in remembrance of my poor mother, Gigella. It was all she gave me when I left home for Siena. And you, what have you got to remember your mother by?"

When he realized that Pietro wasn't paying attention, he became upset. How could a son possibly act that way! And to think he had wanted to give him his name—wanted so much for his son to be like him, to be part of him!

He had half a mind to pick him up and snap him in two like a stick! Why, of all people, did his son refuse to bend to his wishes? Wasn't he supposed to mind even more than the others?

Suddenly, as though in response to an insidious whisper, it came to Domenico that nothing made him different from anyone else.

If that were so, it would have been better had Pietro never been born! Why had he been born? Better not even speak to him any more, but just let him walk along without a word, head lolling until it hit the pavement.

Since the restaurant staff was waiting in the street, Pietro took the keys and went in with them. But he refused to stay afterwards the way he was supposed to and went home instead. When he handed him the keys, Domenico hadn't even looked at him. But after he finished the shopping, he called and gave him a scolding for leaving the staff unsupervised.

"You'll never learn to be boss. How can you ever give orders if you can't follow them yourself?"

Even though he had brooded about this for a long time, he spoke kindly. He held up the bunches of birds for the cooking spit. "This is a thrush," he said, "and this is a lark. Come help me with the plucking."

And he sat down in front of the big feather basket. But Pietro was so uninterested he started to hum.

"If it's all right with you," he said finally, "I'm going to go read a book."

After Domenico finished skewering the plucked birds, he got the turning mechanism ready. "What book?" he asked.

"Even if I told you, you wouldn't know what it is."

"I'm your father," said Domenico gravely, raising one hand in his superior manner, "and I know more about it than all the experts. Nobody knows what's right for you better than I do."

As if to prove he was right, he put one hand on his chest—right on the bloody, feather-covered apron. Then he went to the stove, took the shovel and broke up a clinker; he grabbed Tiburzi by the shoulder and shoved his face down next to the coal hole.

"Can't you see the fire's gone out?" he shouted.

By now Domenico had forgotten about Pietro. When he realized he was still standing there, he went and shook his fist in his face.

"Clear out of here!"

Head hanging, Pietro just stood looking at him.

Not even the cooks' hustle and bustle, jerked around by Domenico's shoves and insults as he called for all the main dishes to be ready immediately, could break him out of his distraction.

By now the restaurant-keeper's boorishness had cowed everyone into silence. They all did what they were told, though perhaps with more mistakes than otherwise. But when Domenico himself took the extra pieces of meat to the cubbyhole for storage, Guerrino turned quickly to Pietro and stuck out his tongue: a reminder of one of the previous night's stories. Though they went on working, everyone laughed.

"Tell me another story," said Pietro softly.

The cook, who was trying to cope with a slippery piece of ham rind, motioned for him to wait. Tiburzi, his navy-blue jacket bunched over his apron ties, was watching them carefully, but just with his eyes, his head motionless; he thought it was hilarious and kept tapping his feet merrily, his arms in the greasy dish-pan with the dirty dishes and tepid water. He had a hard, yellowish goiter that seemed to have a stone stuck in it—one of those stuffed chicken goiters.

Though Domenico often pretended he hadn't seen or heard what was going on, hoping in this way to find out what his staff was up to, this time he came right back. "Ghisola's been corrupting you too!" he said.

"Why?" asked Pietro, surprised and apprehensive.

Everyone turned and grinned curiously.

Why did he think it was her fault? Someone had fed him a lot of lies! That was why he had sent her back to Radda! But he still liked her and wanted to see her again. He hated the unfair way they made fun of her. Why did everyone look at him so maliciously and laugh and joke about it? And why was his father so sure of himself? He stood there unhappily, his outstretched fingers pressing on the table.

By this time he was a pale, slender young man with the unpleasant habit of holding one shoulder higher than the other. He dressed shabbily, a piece of red ribbon around his invariably dirty and wrinkled collar. His hair was blond, his ears were too big and stuck out too far from his head; his eyes were an extremely light blue with something defensive about them. He wore an expression of ingenuous and melancholy rancor that was confident and brave, half-embarrassed, and quite unpleasant.

He would seem depressed for days on end; but once someone spoke to him, he calmed down immediately, became quite affable, and didn't stammer so much.

His feelings about many things were still extremely puzzling and this made him unhappy. Spring was like an assault on his senses. To read a book, then, under a tree! He would stop reading anywhere he wanted, in the middle of the page, get up, pull down a branch, and all but rub his face in it. It was almost as if he were trying to ask permission—seeing, as he did, the hill in front of him with a cascade of white flowers covering it, almond and peach trees curving down as if trying to spread out on the ground. He looked to see if anyone were watching, sighed, and went back to his reading. But he had yet to discover the book that would speak to his heart. Sometimes the pages seemed to lose all consistency and turn so transparent he could see right through them. Then he would have to stop reading.

He would also stop if a bug crawled up his leg and got onto the book.

Sometimes a bird would land inside the flowering branches, threading through them just as surely and confidently as a needle— as if the foliage had opened and closed just for its sake.

Even before Anna died, he refused to go to church; she could hardly ever get him to pray. He was sure he was an atheist. And he cursed too—just to show what little stock he put in priestly superstitions. Domenico blamed it all on those damned school books.

At Poggio a' Meli Domenico was having the stock castrated. The way the farmhands joked about it, Giacco and Masa were sure they were alluding to their granddaughter.

"Good! That'll keep them from running away. And they'll fatten up good too."

Sometimes there were as many as a dozen gloomy new capons with bloody feathers pecking listlessly at their feed. Out in the barn the yearlings, whose eyes were darker and sadder than usual, were still stunned and in pain from the operation.

The dog stretched out in the farmyard and the silent, embittered cats crouched wide-eyed under the wagon or behind the bundles of kindling.

Now they had chosen a male kitten for the restaurant and were taking him away from his mother. The gelder seized him, stuck his head in a sack clamped tight between his knees, and made a quick slash with his belt knife. Instead of falling tangled into the sack, the animal gave a yowl, sprang off, and disappeared.

"That's that. He almost forgot to go miaow!"

"Not much to it at that."

And they all laughed in admiration.

Domenico, partly to emphasize his own disdain, was standing to one side. "What do I owe you?" he said to the man.

"A lira. Or is that too much?"

"A lira?"

"Pay me whatever you want. You always have to do things your own way anyhow!"

He had had a stroke that had left his mouth contorted and his bleary eyes watered constantly.

"I'll give you half a lira and a plate of spaghetti at the restaurant."

And he counted out the money.

Grimacing in malevolent displeasure, the man bounced the coins in the palm of his hand for a moment, checked to make sure they were sound, and then stuffed them into his pocket.

"Just so there's plenty of spaghetti!"

Glancing at the farmhands who had come back for dinner, he gave Domenico a pat on the stomach. "Just look how fat the rich get," he said.

But Carlo put a finger across his lips and they all pretended they hadn't heard.

"What happened to the cat?" asked Pietro. "Shall I go look for him?"

"Leave him alone. He'll come back when he gets hungry."

"He won't die, will he?" he asked the gelder.

"Don't worry about that. He'll lick the wound until it heals. They take better care of themselves than we do."

Then they began to talk about the other castrations—especially Toppa's. Whenever other dogs came around, he would put his tail between his legs and growl. When they looked at him, he slunk away as if he had understood. But he came back later when they were finishing their dinners and gossiping through their open doors across the yard as the women finished up inside.

"Draw me a pitcher of water, Adele," said Carlo, coming out from where he had been standing.

She did as she was told, leaving the pitcher on the well where the chain for hoisting the bucket was still swaying.

Not one of the hands had taken his eyes off her. Now they each took a drink, one at a time, soaking their slices of hard bread in the water afterwards.

One eye peeled for the master, who had gone to check on the livestock, they ambled through the carriage yard discussing the field work.

Pietro had stayed behind and was enjoying watching them eat. One was throwing back his head and nibbling the bread from the palm of his hands so as not to waste the crumbs.

Carlo was stout and husky, even if he did have leg pains all winter. The coarse linen shirt he wore was always extremely clean, though he stank of manure and invariably had the garlic and onions he was so fond of on his breath. Whenever he bit into his bread he would stare at the teeth marks left from the previous bite.

The gelder assumed that Carlo was more important than the other hands; before leaving, he showed him the money he had earned.

"See these coins? They're just like people: some made one way, some made another. This one has been hammered so hard you can hardly tell what it is. This one is bent like a cripple; this has a hole like when you stick or get stuck with a knife. And this one's so worn it only weighs half what it should. It's a poor soul just like I am and to get it off my mind I am going to use it to buy my first drink. Be seeing you."

He spat and gave an oath.

Carlo barely answered. But once the man was out of earshot, he said, "He was trying to get some of my bread for his lunch. But it didn't work."

And he turned to look at his house where the bread-chest still lay open.

Three years had gone by and Pietro had finished the technical school. After enormous trouble and a great deal of resistance, he had finally gone back and settled down to study.

He spent all his free time with his schoolmates and Domenico even let them come into the restaurant to get him.

But it was in this period that he began to discover women. He would sneak out to them, raising the money by selling his school-books and whatever else he could slip out of the house without Domenico's knowing: a set of ceramic dishes, some medallions with good stones, even an antique silk and ivory fan. When he got back he would replace the house keys under the crocheted coaster where they kept the lamp.

One of the day-hands at Poggio a' Meli had fallen in love with Rebecca and he let it be known he was ready to marry her. For some time now Rosi had been having one of Ghisola's cousins, a girl who was also Rebecca's niece, come in from Radda; he figured that he could let them get married and then give the niece her aunt's job. So he put up her dowry, paid some of the wedding expenses, and even hired the groom as a waiter.

After Anna's death Rebecca had stayed on good terms with the master. But Rosaura, the niece, quickly took her place in his sympathies, and aunt and niece bickered constantly, right up until the wedding, even in the restaurant. This upset Giacco and Masa because they were afraid their old-age security was being put in jeopardy.

Masa didn't want anyone to know how much she was loafing and tried to keep out of sight. She was worried they were going to turn her out, especially since she knew the master better than the others and didn't trust him much. When she sat down she would hoist up her skirt, pull down her white cotton stockings and massage the pains in her legs.

The other women, who were working just as hard as ever, resented what was happening and hoped she would get caught, even going so far as to accuse her of stealing. But they would cover up for her too, since they also wanted to keep on her good side.

But she stayed in Domenico's favor since she was the one who kept him informed about the farm.

Giacco, however, no longer asked Pietro for cigarette butts. Indeed, he no longer approved of him and even complained to the master, saying that if it hadn't been for him, a poor old man nobody respected, everything at Poggio a' Meli would have been stolen, right on down to the bricks in the farmyard—and with his son's connivance too.

"He's just not sensible! If you don't mind my saying . . . That is, excuse me if I do say so. And why does he dislike me so?"

Domenico would calm him down as best he could—though he was careful not to overdo it. Giacco would pretend to be hurt and insulted, making believe that he had said more than he meant to.

Sometimes, when he was trying to garner sympathy, he would take off his hat and slap it across his knee. "I just don't have any luck," he would exclaim, in obvious reference to Pietro.

But by now he no longer worked with the others, doing only what used to be his niece's job. His legs had grown so crooked they knocked together and looked like two tangled bell ropes.

When he started to talk, his big head would wobble on his bent and withered shoulders. His face was indescribable: the skin stiff from a stroke and the sunburnt, laniard-like wrinkles filled with grease and dirt. His mouth had disappeared beneath a tangled, drooping moustache that looked like some kind of animal hair. His lower eyelids were swollen and yellowish.

Before doing anything, he always scratched behind his ear, holding his hat up high with his other hand as if deep in thought.

When the little master went by, he would pluck him by the sleeve. "Aren't you even talking to me any more?"

Pietro was avoiding him. He couldn't stand this hypocrisy; it only showed how much more important than Pietro he thought he was.

When he did make him stop, he would adopt a suspicious tone that was meant to be affectionate. "I've known you since you were a baby that I used to dandle on my knee . . . You're not angry with me, are you?"

If Pietro would smile at this, he would feel that the time invested had been worthwhile.

"Why don't you like me?" he began again in a gloomy and resentful tone, as if trying to persuade him of something.

Although Pietro was flattered by this wheedling, he could scarcely find it in him to answer.

"Anyway, I've always done my duty and your father knows it. And as long as God keeps me going, I'll keep on doing it."

And then his tone would get arrogant.

This exaggerated obstinance revolted Pietro.

When he stared at him that way, Pietro would avert his eyes and hurry off.

Giacco would try to make him smile, stopping when he realized from Pietro's expression that he wasn't succeeding. But Pietro would be relieved and feel free to go.

"What do you hear from Ghisola?" he asked one day.

The question pleased Giacco because now he could see a way to get the little master onto his side. Nonetheless, he hesitated before pressing his advantage.

"Oh, I haven't heard a thing about her for quite a while."

"But where is she?"

There were a number of things Giacco might have told him. But instead of answering, he began to scratch at his chest. Through his torn shirt you could see his huge, dark nipples with swollen pores and long hairs all over them. There was a crease around his neck made by a filthy cord attached to a little bag of medals.

"She's at Radda, I think," he said quietly, pointing with his sickle toward the Chianti hills.

"Do you still have the letter?"

"The wife's took it. I guess she's kept it. At least I imagine she has. By God, she better not have thrown it away!" he added, though making it clear he thought she hadn't.

"Why should she have thrown it away?" Pietro asked. "If you still care about her, you should still have the letter. I want to see it."

He listed these things as though they were rights he was compelled to defend. The old man was getting more and more on his nerves. Giacco hesitated, but was curious as well.

"She sent something else too," he announced, winking.

"What? I bet it's her picture."

"Who told you?" Giacco laughed, clapping him on the shoulder and then quickly pulling back his hand.

"Did she? Tell me!"

Delighted, Giacco leaned back against an olive tree before continuing.

"That's what she did!" he said.

He looked like a turtle who has made certain no one will bother him and is about to inch forward again.

Silent but content, Pietro started to walk to the old man's house. Radda wasn't far away at all!

The ears of wheat had been bent by the wind and rain until they looked like hooks of pale gold; the stalks were all ruffled and some were broken.

"Wait, listen to me . . ." Giacco called.

Masa was sitting on the bedroom stoop drying the dishes.

"Your husband told me you have a letter from Ghisola. Is that true?"

The old woman had often thought about letting him read it and told him the truth without hesitation.

"Did he really tell you?" she said.

"Have you got any objections?"

When she bent over to let him pass, he didn't wait for her to straighten up again but shoved right into the bedroom.

Although she told as many tales to the master as Giacco did, he liked Masa better.

"I'll be right there. Don't start going through that bureau. You won't find it."

"Hurry up," he snapped. "You're just ignorant and don't understand how I feel about her."

He was worried that Giacco, who intimidated him, was going to come back. The looks Giacco shot him sometimes made him nervous, though not more prudent.

Masa did find the letter. Before handing it over, she clutched it against her sunken chest. "I don't want the master to know anything about this," she said.

"Why should he? Who's going to tell him?"

"You ought to know that better than I do," she answered, reddening.

She bit her lips, making the same nibbling gesture she used when she was trying to thread a needle.

It bothered him that the envelope had been pinched open along the seam: all that to get at a letter that Ghisola, who couldn't write, must have dictated to a relative. Pietro read it out loud from beginning to end: her parents had had the measles; Aunt Giuseppa couldn't nurse the baby; and so on.

"Where's the photograph?" he demanded.

Masa was laughing in satisfaction and running her fists over her hips. When she laughed you could see her white, close-set teeth.

"It's been behind the bureau ever since it fell there more than a week ago when I was trying to dust."

Under a row of saints that were hanging from a string on the wall he could see an old frame made of navy-blue velvet, but it was empty. The blank space with the white paper in it moved him deeply.

"Didn't it occur to you to try to get it out before this?"

It was clear he was about to to see it. He was only doing his duty.

But Masa was in no mood to be scolded. "What's the hurry!" she said. "And when do we have time for things like that? In the morning we get up early and at night we're too tired."

"I'll move the bureau."

When there was something that mattered to him he would pitch in and help out too!

"Don't you try to rattle me!"

But the usual malice had gone from her eyes, replaced by a murky, ambiguous sweetness.

"What do you mean?"

"The bureau is heavy. You might hurt yourself and the master would blame it on me."

When she said things like that about him, Pietro felt like disappearing into a hole.

"Come help me then."

By now they were on the brink of an argument. Instead, moving slowly and taking the pieces one at a time, she began to remove the bricabrac: a chipped porcelain vase that had contained who knows how many flowers; a bell jar with a wax image of Saint Catherine; a broken sliver of greenish mirror.

"Just a minute."

As he pulled at the worm-eaten bureau, the picture that had been stuck to the wall fell out. Eyes riveted to the photograph and feeling as terrified as if he had almost been hit by lightning, he picked it up and carried it to the window.

"Do you see how beautiful she's grown? You're sure to really like her now!"

Pietro could see what she meant by beautiful. He was overcome with happiness and his heart was thumping. Though his lips were trembling, he couldn't utter a word.

Masa didn't understand what was going on or what was about to happen. She stared at him intently, her eyelids fluttering.

Then she punched him on the arm. "What are you going to do with it?" she asked.

She was afraid he was going to take it with him, though Pietro, worried that Ghisola wouldn't approve, would never have dared to do this.

"Just keep it here in the frame," he said in a changed voice. "That's what I want. Don't let it fall down again either."

Masa was happy to comply. Taking a rag, she cleaned the cobwebs from the wall and then Pietro put back the photograph and replaced the bureau.

"Keep the letter too."

"Really, if she had behaved more decently toward us, we'd feel better about her."

When Pietro started at this, in a way she had never seen before, she added, "But I still like her as much as I always did."

"What has she ever done to you? I'd like to know what she could have done to you? You're making it up!"

"I can't tell you. It's my own business and that's all I'll say."

Having her granddaughter sent away was a reflection on her too! She nibbled repeatedly at her lower lip.

"Don't you go and say anything. And don't tell anyone, not even Rebecca, that I showed it to you. Get on out of here; if anyone even suspects, there's going to be trouble."

As soon as he left he knew that he was in love with Ghisola, and that there was nothing strange or unpleasant about it—quite the opposite. If only he were more certain, he could have told Masa immediately, explaining about the principal of social retribution and how he was offering himself willingly. Why shouldn't she be rich too?

Three days later he went back to Poggio a' Meli.

The shadow of a pear tree lay light and motionless on the sun-drenched barn. The stripes the shadow made seemed like fever measurements that were throbbing like boiling water or his own veins.

On the shed roof grew a sempervivum plant almost six feet in diameter. It drooped down so far you could see how one shoot was jammed into the next and the stem scarcely sufficient to hold up the blossom and prickly leaves. There were a straw flask cover and a pair of rusty sickles up there too plus a little bottle lying between two stones to get the sun; in it was a scorpion and some oil that Carlo was saving for putting on cuts.

Pietro noticed a faded rag that had been plastered by the rain onto the roof peak: half of one of Ghisola's old petticoats.

He went looking for Masa. "Let me see that picture again," he demanded.

But now he was worried that the old lady would be angry and maybe write her granddaughter and he only glanced at it quickly.

Mount Amiata looked made out of liquid and about to flood down to the ground.

Pietro was delicate and frequently ill and Domenico found him repulsive. Pale and thin, he was little more than a common idiot, and no help in the business either!

When he would put his finger on the smooth distended veins in his slender neck, Pietro would hang his head and want to apologize. But such submissiveness made no sense to a violent nature like Domenico's, irritating him instead and making him want to mock him.

Those books! How he longed to grind them beneath his heel! Sometimes, catching sight of his son with a book in his hand, he would lose patience, seize the book, and slap him across the face with it.

People who wrote books were nothing more than swindlers—they would never get a meal on tab at his restaurant!

Even so, Pietro had got him to pay his technical school tuition for three years running!

Once he had given him an inspection—checking his ears, maybe, or the weak empty spot behind his neck—Domenico would start to gesture like an animal, stop eating, gnaw his lower lip, and suddenly stick his knife into the middle of the table.

Though Pietro was quiet and kept out of his way, he refused to obey. He was home very little, waiting, when he needed school money, until a customer that Domenico respected—someone he would never say no in front of—came in. He had learned to take it, to put up with everything without a whimper. School for him, more than anything else, was an excuse to keep away from the restaurant.

Since sarcastic hostility was all he ever saw there, he never even looked for affection in his father's eyes.

But how to avoid him? If he looked at him just once with a less than cowed expression, Domenico would push his fist—a fist capable of hoisting a whole barrel of wine—into his face. If Pietro smiled shakily, declaring that, "One day I'll be as strong as you are," Domenico would roar in that voice of his: "You?"

Frightened and disgusted, Pietro would duck his head and slowly push the fist away.

When he was little, that voice used to terrify and sicken him so much that, instead of crying, he would crouch down at the sound and hide where they couldn't bother him. Hearing it now made him uneasy, exasperated. He knew he didn't have to suffer like this and grew even more indignant when he saw words like "justice" and "redemption" in the propaganda leaflets that his barber lent him.

He became a member of the socialist party, even founding a local youth chapter. Though secretive at first, later he began to brag about it with everyone who came to the restaurant. It had become his ambition to write articles for the weekly edition of *The Class Struggle*. He didn't care if the police did arrest him. His dreams were filled with trials, martyrdom, speeches, even revolution. If someone called him "comrade" he would do anything he wanted.

Domenico, for his part, was more and more preoccupied with the business and the farm. And he had no one to help him!

In the suffocating heat when nobody was in the restaurant, the cook and dishwasher would take a nap. They would lay their heads on the chopping block with their aprons up to protect them from the flies that buzzed over the greasy dishrags, landed on the table next to a spot of broth, and then sashayed up and down rubbing themselves against the chunks of meat. The copper saucepan would start to boil and under the table a cat would be gnawing at something while a half-closed brass faucet would drip and hiss. The transparent reflections thrown against the wall by the water in the two dishpans were crisscrossed now and again by the shadow of a fly.

If a customer arrived, the waiter would grab a plate from the pile and yell for the cook.

"That's the end of your nap."

The sweat built up beneath his shirt would suddenly turn chill and he would scratch an ear that had been caught between his head and his arms and gone all pins and needles.

The restaurant was coming back to life.

Pietro spent his vacation time reading, hardly aware of the hours that passed. Domenico would creep in on tiptoe and catch him at it.

"Why aren't you keeping an eye on the help?"

And the scolding would begin.

"Come help weigh the straw," he bellowed in his ear one day.

"Me?"

"You."

Grabbing him by the collar, he pulled him out of the chair. But then, in a hurry, he rushed out to where the straw-sellers were waiting. Holding his head against a corner of the wall, Pietro stood motionless, disgusted at the tears welling up inside him.

"Here's some more, boss!" said one of the two men who had helped with the previous load.

"That's a lot of straw!" another yelled from where he was pulling on a rope attached to the wagon.

"It'll go a ton," added Pallaccola, who was holding the wagon shafts.

Their exaggerations made the restaurant-keeper smile. After feeling and sniffing at the straw, he glared at them both without responding.

Two more men were waiting in the courtyard outside the kitchen; they were tired and sweaty from unloading and hoisting the bales into the stable loft. Leaning with their backs against the wall, they sat squatting on their heels. The sweat dripped off their foreheads onto the cracked and swollen toes of their dusty shoes.

"How much do you want?" the restaurant-keeper asked, thumbs in his vest pockets and sucking from time to time at a scratch on the back of his hand.

"How much is it worth to you? We have to make a living too," Ceccaccio answered.

"We don't get anything for nothing from those filthy peasants," added Palloccola. "We almost killed ourselves."

Arriving just at threshing time so the peasants would be glad to hand over a forkful of straw just to get rid of them, they had made the rounds from farm to farm. The peasants were afraid that if they said no, they would steal even more out of spite and so nobody refused to give them some straw.

They didn't have jobs but made a living more by stealing than by working.

Domenico was laying in a huge supply at the lowest prices: enough to keep the stable in straw for the rest of the year.

"You want to weigh it or go by eye?" Domenico asked, removing his thumbs from his pockets.

"Whatever you think. Whatever you decide is all right with us."

"Meanwhile, you can let us go," interrupted Pipi and Nosse, who had already come to an understanding with him. "Pay us our money."

They were both young, Pipi with a broad forehead, an enormous, swollen head, and gentle, deep blue eyes as tender as a baby's. Nosse had a black moustache and black eyes so lively they looked as if they might bite.

"Give us a hand getting this straw up first."

"If there's a drink in it, we'll help you," said Pipi, laughing and spitting on the wall.

"My throat's all dusty," said Nosse, bracing himself as he got up from the wall for the last time.

Domenico smiled and agreed.

By this time he was already more than fifty years old. His hands had turned pale and had prominent, reddish violet veins and long, narrow fingernails that were curled at the edges.

His whiskers were blond, almost white, and he didn't shave nearly as often as he did in the past. His eyes were as shiny as oyster shells, though the edges of the lids were swollen and lined with purple. Even though he kept it slicked with a juniper lotion of his own concoction, his hair was getting thinner. His moustache was tight on his cheeks and bristly around a mouth that was almost affable.

His walk had become more stooped and his shoulders were thicker, but he still weighed more than two hundred pounds and was proud of being as strong as ever. His wrists and neck especially, he felt, were invincible, something he needed to protect and keep in shape for when he needed them.

"By weight then?" asked Ceccaccio.

"It won't go two hundred," the restaurant-keeper retorted.

"What do you mean?" shouted Ceccaccio. "Three hundred pounds."

"We're honest folk," added Palloccola, cursing.

But they hurried over to unload the straw. Going to the wagon, Domenico lifted the straw by the binding and, knees bent for added power, pressed it high in the air.

"I'll give you four liras and even that's too much."

"We stole it anyway, didn't we, Ceccaccio?"

Laughing at first, they ended up cursing and shouting.

"Pay us then; we want to get going."

"Don't you want anything to drink?" the stablekeeper asked coldly from up in the loft.

"No, no. We're too tired. We can't help you hoist it."

"Look what muscles!" said Pipi, taking Domenico by the arm where his shirt was rolled up.

"Some arms!" Nosse exclaimed.

"Come on up, boys," said Ceccaccio.

You could see the street from the half-open door and when a girl went by, Ceccaccio whistled.

"Wait and see if she's coming this way," said Pipi.

"What's going on?" demanded the restaurant-keeper. "Are you standing here so you can fool around?"

"What are we doing here?" And Ceccaccio's pal flopped down, hands on knees, onto the straw.

"Weren't you in a rush a minute ago?"

"That's right. Pay up."

"Here's six liras. Now clear out!"

Pipi and Nosse got into their wagon and left.

"Now it's up to us."

"How much are we going to get for it?"

"Let's weigh it."

Setting the balance hook on a pole, they put the loop in the rope through the hook.

"Weigh it up, master!"

"No leaning your knee on it."

"Me? Look—I'm a yard from it."

Placing the pole on his shoulder and with his whole body trembling at the effort, Palloccola lifted both hands over his head.

The load weighed two hundred pounds. They figured the bill and bound the straw so they could raise it up with the block and tackle.

"Are you helping too, master?"

"I'm doing more than you are; I've got stronger arms."

All of them grabbed the rope from where it dangled from the upper pulley. Domenico wrapped it around his wrist and the wooden pulley squealed as showers of dust and pieces of straw fell on the men below and the bundle began to rise in the air. One hand stretched out, the stablekeeper was leaning out of the loft. Those hoisting bent down with one breath and the bundle revolved slowly over their heads. As soon as the stableman could reach it, it disappeared into the darkness.

"That's that," said Ceccaccio, knocking some dust and bits of straw from his neck. But he felt as sore in the arms as if someone had been yanking on them.

The restaurant-keeper had suddenly become suspicious about something; he walked over to a pile of broken bricks and scraps of metal.

"There's an old lock missing," he said. "Who took it?"

The two straw-sellers looked at each other for a moment; then they went back to winding their ropes.

"Who took the lock, boys?" repeated Domenico, by now quite pale.

"Not me for sure," said Ceccaccio calmly.

"I didn't say it was you. I only said someone took it."

"What do we need a thing like that for?" said Palloccola, disgusted and resentful.

"Pipi probably took it! That's his line of work!" Ceccaccio said laughing.

"I don't know if it is or not. But if I did, I'd get it back. This is nothing to brag about."

By now the two men were beginning to feel apprehensive; each of them was worried that the other was the thief.

"Go on and search us!" Palloccola shouted.

"I'm not searching anyone! Here's your money. But this is the last time I buy any straw from you!"

"We don't know anything about it!"

Domenico could see there was no way to find out who had really done it and assumed that the four of them were in cahoots. So he waved them away and went back into the restaurant.

"If you'd kept your eye on things the way I told you," he said to Pietro, grabbing him by the collar again, "they wouldn't carry things off on you."

"They only steal because they're poor," thought Pietro shrugging his shoulders. And he sidled off, filled with the dread he always felt when his father was about to hit him. Domenico was going to lunge at him, but Rosaura held him back.

The lock had been taken by a passing beggar the day before.

That evening, exhausted from work but their bellies filled with convent food, all three men fell asleep drunk in a tavern—all except Pipi, who slept at home with his wife.

The restaurant had only one entrance when Rosi took over *The Blue Fish*, the one on Via dei Rossi where the metal pennant with the painted fish on its sides was attached. Above the doorway there was a relief of a fifteenth-century Madonna, its votive light still attached though without the cord for raising and lowering it.

The additional two entrances from the Via Cavour were added later. Just past one of these was the double-decked plate-glass display case filled with plucked chickens, different kinds of roasts, and other delicious things arranged on lining paper that they changed every week.

On the other side of the Via dei Rossi entrance there was a large door that led into a small courtyard that was always crowded with buggies and other carriages. Then came the stable with room for thirty horses and a large loft above it.

On Saturdays Domenico would distribute the leftover bread to the poor.

At the beginning of the Via dei Rossi where they had the old entrance, the street is quite narrow; a whole hour before the distribution it would begin to fill with beggars. Pipi's wife would be among them: a woman still young but so drained and yellow that her mouth seemed a lipless slit. She walked as though incapable of looking to one side or the other and you could frequently catch sight of her flat, breastless chest through her dirty, carelessly buttoned dress.

There was also an old woman with an enormous purple nose and a straw farmhat so badly unravelled it always had one less round of straw on its brim. She insisted on the first portion and refused to leave until the last crust was distributed.

Once in a while she would start to scream: "That old bitch got more than I did!"

Propping her stick under her arm, she would open up her kerchief and check the crusts again.

One beggar woman came three times a week to get bread from Domenico. She was big and had a face like a mask of red skin that she couldn't take off. Winter and summer she wore a black shawl that was tied behind her back while she kept her pale hands crossed on her chest. Her daughter, who was tall and pretty, stuck tight to her side, one hand under her elbow. She was feeble-minded and always had a sweet, warm smile on her face.

The two of them would brush against the walls and move in long strides as if they were trying to get away from something. Whenever they had to cross the street they would scurry even faster.

When they went to a convent to get the free soup, the daughter would turn and guffaw silently each time she withdrew the spoon from her mouth.

They put her in the madhouse after her mother died.

There was also a blind man and his son who had a paralyzed hand and a missing finger. "Why don't you help me, you loafer!" the father would yell. "You'll never get us bread if you lean against the wall like that. Good for nothing! Bum!"

Wondering how much bread was left, he would cup a hand behind his ear, all in the same tone he used in his prayers.

The remaining poor would flock around Rosaura like chickens around spilled corn.

The blind man's son stood listening, picking at the mortar between the bricks. He knew Rosaura would save him something without his fighting and he wanted to be last.

All the women examined the bread that was distributed to them; some would leave the hardest crusts next to the entrance in a hollow in the wall.

Whenever she noticed this, Rosaura would stick out her head and exclaim, "Just look at her! First she begs for bread and then she's too good for it."

"I'd have eaten it if it had come my way!" said a woman who was standing arms akimbo.

Laughing, another woman bit hard into a crust she had been massaging in her filthy hands. Suddenly, in the midst of their barely audible murmuring, an argument exploded.

"Even though she's rich, she still comes begging for bread."

"What's it to you? I'm rich, am I? Well, that's none of your business."

"If you can't keep quiet," interjected Rosaura, "I won't give you any more bread."

"She's right," answered another, her face disfigured by a rash that she hid under a blue rag neckerchief tied at the back of her head. "But you don't hear me complaining."

All you could see were her inflamed eyes like double wounds that wouldn't stay open. She turned her head when she wanted to look at something and whenever she talked the bandage moved in time with her mouth. And what a mouth it was!

An old man, who almost never arrived until the bread was gone, was using that wheedling tone that beggars are fond of when they want to make you feel sorry for them.

"Some for me too—for the love of God."

"There isn't any more. Why didn't you come earlier?"

"My legs just don't hold me up any longer!"

And he would whack his stick on a doorstep.

"They managed to get you here now, however," answered Rosaura, going back inside without giving him anything.

Furious and determined, he would keep on waiting.

"Please ma'am. Don't make me suffer any more."

He had worked hard all his life and would dream of getting sick, entering the hospital, and then spending the whole day in bed and eating well too!

At least his wife had died young and was no longer suffering. He had begun to consider free bread his right: a thing like a doorstep that nobody can take away once you're sitting on it.

Domenico never did remarry. He thought about it a lot, however, scratching his half-shaved chin hard with his fingernails, pinching the skin at his throat, and rapping things softly with his knuckles. When he got angry, he would be sure to announce he was about to do it.

"You're the one who ought to be getting married!" he would say to Pietro, thinking he would want to safeguard his interests and not have a stepmother around. "But you have to play the socialist, you imbecile! Aren't you ashamed?"

Once a year he bought a new hat and wore it every day until the brim, which he always kept jammed on his ears, was completely soiled. He wore his shirts two weeks at a stretch and cursed and swore whenever it was time to buy a new one. He was so determined to hang onto his hard-won social position that he made foolish efforts to save money—though he was quick to tell others how foolish they were. He even expected their admiration. "I've made my money by the sweat of my brow and I intend to hang on to it."

He was supersitious too, especially about a religious medal that the farmhands had found while spading. He kept the medal with some copper coins in a wooden bowl. Whenever he wanted to examine it—which is to say, every time he came across it—he had to put on his glasses.

Since he could take his fingernail and scratch its surface until it looked like new, he liked this medal. When they brought him the glasses he had been searching all over for, he would sit and polish them with his smelly, red handkerchief.

"I can't see it very well."

He would show it to the grocer, the drygoods dealer, and the barber, his nearest accessible friends.

Naturally, they didn't know what kind of medal it was either.

Sometimes he would take off his hat and lean against the shop doorway saying hello to people he scarcely knew.

They would bring him a chair in the summer and he would sit snoozing in it until someone who was passing slapped his thigh and woke him.

"I just dozed off for a minute," he would say resentfully.

He would shake off his drowsiness by barking some orders.

In a single day he devoured all the overripe fruit.

"Hand me the saucepan," he would shout at the cook, a man whose black hair came almost down to his eyebrows.

Taking a taste, he would shake him by the arm.

"There isn't enough pepper. When will you learn to work by yourself?"

The man who had been scolded shrugged his shoulders resentfully.

"Bring me the other pan."

The man did it and then stood watching, one hand on the table.

Domenico didn't even wait to swallow before he started to shout. "You've burnt the garlic."

"Either I can never leave you alone in the kitchen or else I have to fire you," he concluded, wiping his moustache in a napkin. "Real men just aren't born any more."

Every morning he would eat all the previous day's leftovers from the serving dishes in the pantry.

And he would drink almost a whole flask of wine, turning to the wall when he was finished and belching into his handkerchief. The fumes made him tipsy and talkative, though everything outside the kitchen seemed a waste of time—everything but Poggio a' Meli.

Once he had finished the first part of his course in Siena on his own, Pietro was permitted to go to the Florence technical school. This meant a complete break between father and son. More and more they were treating each other like strangers forced to live together. Domenico gave up trying to influence him, figuring that this would make Pietro sorry. He was utterly incapable of forgiving his son. For almost a month he made light of it, but his jokes frequently grew into quarrels.

Pietro was still a socialist, even if he didn't spend as much time as before with the workers. It ashamed and humiliated him to be twenty years old and so far behind in his studies.

In Florence he lived in a rented room on Via Cimabue and took his meals at a nearby restaurant.

Head in hand, he would sit for hours, dreaming he was studying, his anxiety crisscrossed by ill humour and melancholy as if by lines made with a T-square.

He was trying to reconcile himself to the situation and work up enthusiasm for school, but the days seemed so separate and disconnected he was overwhelmed by discouragement. He couldn't seem to get his bearings or remember what had happened the previous day, let alone what would happen in the days to come.

He was not doing as well as he'd hoped, not even now that he was committed to his task, and he studied less and less!

Under his window was a convent that had a walled garden where nearly a hundred little girls would play and sing in the early afternoon. What a dreary racket they raised! But then he hated the nuns as well!

When the girls came to the corner nearest his building, he would smile sardonically, hoping they would notice. But they weren't the slightest bit interested and this ended up annoying him too.

You couldn't even hear the noise of the city up there because the convent wall, which ran perpendicular to that of his building, was long and butted into another building so enormous it shut out Piazza Beccaria almost completely. In a semicircle on each side there were other, lower houses blocking everything else.

He was always ill at ease and couldn't figure out why. He couldn't confide in his friends and this upset him too. Everything bothered him. It filled him with a discouraging weariness when he was in Piazza dell'Annunziata after having taken the sun for a few minutes before going back to school and could get a glimpse of the fog-shrouded dome of Santa Maria dei Fiori at the end of the Via dei Servi; the feeling was worse if a bell somewhere was tolling.

Caught up at sundown in dim, distant noises that made him think he was being spied on by air so transparent it frightened and intimidated him, he would feel an immense urge to escape.

When he went to eat it would be almost dusk, the carnival stalls under the trees in Piazza Beccaria blindingly illuminated by acetylene lanterns while a merry-go-round whirled endlessly and barrel-organ music played.

Via Ghibellina and Via dell'Agnolo were so narrow they seemed crushed between the buildings that stood alongside them while near the Barriera Aretina other streets came to an end in the open country under the trees.

When he came back, his landlady would be sitting sewing with other ladies he never spoke to.

Meanwhile, there were more and more days when school exhausted him and he felt wrung out as if by a mysterious guilt.

He was well aware that not everyone could go to school!

When he was with the other students, he could sense he had seen more of life than they had; it was easy for him to call them "ragazzi," when he talked to them. But he disapproved of the way they treated the teachers, could never laugh at what they thought was funny, and frequently got annoyed and scolded them.

It was only when he was lying eyes closed on his bed that he felt really good.

He could tell he had failed to grow fond of his schoolmates. The indifference he felt for some of them had been transformed into hostility and enmity. Others, especially the richer ones who snubbed him because he was a socialist, he simply disliked. His classmates thought he was crazy, though most of them liked him.

In the end, he decided to stop struggling with his weariness and quit going to school. When his friends teased him about this, he explained that his father couldn't afford to support him any longer.

It bothered and pleased him to recognize how estranged he had become from them; he couldn't understand why they studied even without being forced to the way he was. More than ever, he wanted to leave.

One day, after four months of school, he decided not to pay his rent with the money his father had just sent him. Instead, without telling anyone, he went back to Siena.

He was welcomed home like someone who has finally come to his senses—even if it was a bit late. Given this welcome, he didn't dare say that he intended to study for the exams on his own. But when he learned from a letter to Rebecca that Ghisola was in Florence, not Radda, and had been living there for some time, he quickly changed plans again.

Domenico's hopes had risen much too high; he was convinced that Pietro's spontaneous return to Siena was an act of repentance that was almost divinely inspired. He was trying to be reasonable.

"Why do you want to live so far away from me—your own father?" he asked. "Doesn't God tell you in your heart that it's wrong?"

When Domenico realized that even now he couldn't make him obey, he simply left him to his own devices, certain that time would be on his side.

Pietro, to keep his conscience clear and justify defying his father, began to study with a satisfaction he had never known before.

By now there were three years of technical school plus all the time he had spent at the seminary, and this changed everything. He felt he was a different person, and that there were still more changes in store.

His socialism had become "intellectual," as he fashionably termed it. He no longer had the same beliefs as when he was trying to win converts. But socialist morality was still the measure for all his feelings.

Those three years seemed to have gone by as quickly as a day and were losing all consistency for him, even mentally—as if he had finally been granted breathing space.

Despite his supposed determination, the exams had increasingly become a pretext he found it impossible to consider either decent or acceptable. He was also growing impatient to see Ghisola; all his hopes in life were now pinned on her.

He would stay in the house for days at a time, staring with his face against the window pane at the narrow blue rectangle between the roofs. With his eyes riveted on that ridiculous, distant blue, he was driven almost into a frenzy. From that perspective the swallows looked black and flew by as if they had been hurled. But still there was someone he didn't know, looking out from high in the farthest window! And then the feeling of emptiness at a solitude that was trapped in one of the oldest and most deserted buildings in Siena, its broken tower looming above the gloomy Arco dei Rossi—a building hemmed in by dark, empty houses pressed tightly together: houses with carved coats of arms that had belonged to vanished and forgotten families; houses with walls six feet thick; tall, arching casements; stifling rooms with permanently closed windows covered with dust and cobwebs thick as rags; and sharply jutting windowsills.

Sometimes, all at once, his mind would return to Florence and Ghisola waiting for him, maybe ready to scold him—a thought that filled him with exaltation—as he thought again of the roaring Arno, the beautiful hills, and the fog that moistened the walls and darkened the cobblestones that seemed made out of patchwork.

When his father spoke to him he would feel sad and resentful and rush away shuddering so as not to hear him, not to see him. Why was there never a word for him? Why did they treat him even now as if they could hardly stand him? Why did he have to make futile attempts to be like the others? What were others like?

He thought again about his schoolmates in Florence, considering them one by one. Was it possible they didn't even remember him?

How long had it been since his mother died? It seemed a hundred years. Since then he had not participated in anything and was completely ignorant of what had been happening.

His eyes, with their mystic gentleness, contrasted immediately and obviously with the lean and evasive lines of his face.

He was overwhelmed by that deep, persistent indefiniteness that had neither name nor motive and after passing left its mark like water that has passed over sand.

He felt inferior to his friends in Siena, bitterly aware of the mistake he had made—a mistake whose consequences would be felt in a future viewed only as arid expiation.

Why had he tried to become a painter? Was a useless effort like that worth losing his self-esteem? Why couldn't he just forget it and believe in himself again?

He tried to console himself by imagining a new and extraordinary existence. But when would it start? Now and again he would lose track of the idea and wonder how he had ever dreamed such a thing.

Though he was almost a fanatic about his sincerity, no one could have known this. He could sense that his friends found him different now that he was back from Florence. He longed to be forgiven for breaking up with them, but was ashamed and sorry that in the past he had been so sincere and eagerly expansive. Once again he could picture the moral humiliations that people had exploited. He had tried to make friends with the stupidest and most idiotic people in Siena, thinking that they were the only ones suitable for someone like him. It was like a duty for him—so much so that he felt guilty about going for a walk without one of them tagging along. But now that he was back from Florence he managed not to speak to anyone and decided bitterly never to see them again!

Although weak and sometimes wrong, he was the kind of young man who stores up enormous energy.

He kept on dreaming of how his emotions should function and would wake up half-pleased with himself, vindicated almost, as though some superior and mysterious entity had moved over onto his side.

He was waiting with bewildered joy for the day he would meet that superior existence that was turning him upside down.

He had no idea what he would manage to say to it, though he imagined that whatever it was would be luminous with goodness, though sometimes he realized that the words he was thinking of were meaningless terms that were running away with his tongue and abducting his soul: hurled and irretrievable words, words like furiously overhoned knives; words that derive a mad pleasure from draining your very essence and then are replaced by insane terror, by stormy days filled with thunderstorms hotter and more dessicating than the dryness they are supposed to drench.

Sometimes he wished that someone would kill him—Ghisola, perhaps, who he could feel was already his and had come back from his past like a delicious temptation.

Toppa had died of old age. They found his body beneath a cart in the farmyard one February morning. He was half frozen to the bricks and when Carlo, who was going to bury him under an olive tree, took the shovel and hit him on the belly it rang like a drum and made everyone laugh.

He had grown irritable after his castration. When he didn't want to be petted, he would first move away and then rush at you afterward if he weren't left alone. He was a mongrel, about eighteen inches tall and his coat was white, though yellow close to the skin. They called him "Toppa" or "Patch" because he had a black spot over one ear.

When Toppa was a puppy and had just been weaned, Domenico tied him to the well stanchion and the hands were told to kick him when he started to whimper.

Later he bought him a collar with brass spikes that they never took off except for his haircuts.

Toppa could hear the horse's harness bell when Domenico was still outside the city at Porta Camollia and he would dash barking into the road. By the time the horse turned to come through the gate, he would be rushing back and forth in front of them. Although most people were able to avoid him, several children who couldn't get out of his way got knocked down.

After meals he would go for a romp in the fields, leaving his trail behind him, especially in the tall grain where you could see his wake from quite a distance. Since the work had to be done over wherever he had been running, at planting time they had to throw rocks at him to keep him away. He loved ripe grapes and was crazy about figs.

The only people who could get him to mind were Domenico and Giacco. With all the others he was either afraid or tried to bite— Ghisola, for example, when she hopped on his back one time.

No other dog could get away with anything when he was around and he killed a number of them, snapping their spines with his teeth. Two others were torn to pieces when they got too close to the food in his dish.

He tolerated cats, however, so long as they kept their distance. But they had to keep off when it was time for his nap in the sun. At such times he would shut one eye and open the other one, open the first and close the other, then rush forward barking deafeningly.

He never like to play, not even when he was a puppy and be-haved differently according to the person he was with, never once making a mistake in this respect. He never obeyed Pietro, who, in turn, never petted him.

So they buried him, telling Rosi first, who remembered that he had only cost two liras; he told them to save the collar. Giacco, feeling that he too was getting old, began to cry.

"This is just what will happen to us," he said to the others, gaz-ing at the animal's body.

"He couldn't have held out much longer," Enrico answered. "What good are you when you're old in this world, anyhow?"

And he glanced to where Carlo was snickering.

But Giacco threw down his hoe.

"I'll hold out longer than you will," he shouted. "Just keep that in mind. See this poor dumb animal? He had a bigger heart than you do!"

"I wasn't talking about you."

"Who were you talking about, then? Even if my brain is a little slow now, I can still tell what's going on . . ."

"Why couldn't he have lived a bit longer?" said Carlo, cursing the dog angrily. "If he did we wouldn't have to fuss with burying him or with arguing about him either. Are you aware it's a dead dog you're fighting over!"

Though Carlo was pretending to be angry, actually he was glad that Giacco had been made to blanch like that without his having even been part of it. Giacco was watching the dog, making sure nobody was heartless or careless enough to step on him.

When Masa came to watch the burial, she hung back from the grave and kept right on eating, even though it upset her.

When the men finished, she gave herself a slap on the belly. "One more bite," she said, "and my guts are going to be so stuffed . . ."

"That's a joke," said Giacco, lifting his head and looking over. "Why don't you get back to work? You'd fall over dead before you'd stop eating! Do you have any idea how furious you make me!"

"What a sorehead!" Masa replied, replacing the bread in her pocket. "Lord knows!"

Then she went back, walking in front of the others and sighing under her breath, "Oh well, oh well!"

She had no idea what they had been saying to her husband.

Domenico had noticed Ghisola's equivocal behaviour; astute and leery of trouble, he took the precaution of sending her away from Poggio a' Meli.

She was only twelve when she had first gone there; when she returned to Radda she was seventeen.

She knew her other relatives virtually by name only and had not seen her two sisters since leaving. Growing up separately, they had not had much chance to become fond of her. They met her just the same at the carriage stop, however, wearing their new shoes and best shawls for the occasion.

She brought them each an imitation gold ring for a present. Once they had kissed her they didn't know what to do next. Walking home, they couldn't decide if she should be between them or not and kept switching places. Finally the younger sister dropped behind. When Ghisola called her to join them, she went off by herself instead, following the grass on the edge of the road and hanging her head so

Ghisola wouldn't catch her looking. The older sister didn't talk much either; in fact, she didn't say anything.

When they got to the house where their parents were waiting, Ghisola burst into tears. But then they had a fine dinner of fried rabbit and a brace of pan-roasted chickens with full, fat ovaries that could have lived longer before being slaughtered. The bread had been baked the same morning.

Borio di Sandro, a widower and family friend who sometimes helped out with money, brought a flask of his best wine and the tipsiness they got from it that first day made them mutually well-disposed.

But Ghisola had no intention of staying there and working like her sisters. When they talked together, they referred to her as "the delicate signorina." She couldn't bear them for very long; whenever she could, she would take to the fields instead. Even though they didn't dislike her, she always managed to keep out of whatever they were trying to discuss. She even went to mass alone, thinking as she did so about Poggio a' Meli. Already she was sorry she had come back to Radda, but only Borio understood. They could kill her if they wanted to, she would say to him, but she wasn't going to stay there.

The following year, on the evening of an big religious holiday, he took her up to a village procession.

The procession was of couples of local peasants following a small cross with their hats in their hands. Then there was a group of girls singing from songbooks they were clutching as if in the teeth of a gale. After this there was another cross: a huge, black, dusty one with a crown of thorns and rope whips dangling down. The priest came last.

Ghisola, who had always felt superior to these people and had never been interested in any of the young men, was escorted home by the widower.

They came back down a steep road that was flanked, before it came out in the fields, by thick cypress rows that grew darker and darker the further from town. The path they took was a rocky one that circled the side of a large, stunted hill with tall oaks on it.

Ghisola, who liked Borio very much, was one step ahead of him. As often happens after the forced and unusual gaiety of a holiday, she was feeling depressed.

"Why has she stopped looking at me?"

By now his cigar had lost its taste; since all it did was increase his confusion, he threw it away. They were completely alone! No telling what had become of the others! Even if there were sometimes footsteps in front, the sound went away immediately.

Ghisola was not watching where she was walking and seemed to be trying to make herself smaller. If it hadn't been for Borio, she might have toppled into a ravine. She listened for his breathing and stuck close to his side.

From time to time she would make a slip; her legs seemed so stiff and elongated that she trembled at every step. She decided she had better stop since she could feel her head spinning and was starting to think she had had too much to drink. Unconsciously, she was taking extremely deep breaths, sucking her stomach way in.

The moon was trembling from beyond a veil of clouds and there were feeble, transparent shadows emerging from the darkness everywhere. For Borio, Ghisola was something weak, almost clownish; when he took her hand, she let him do it. But she knew what was going on! When he kissed her she gave a little jump and pushed him away. He kissed her again, staring afterwards at the back of her neck where there was a groove between her shoulder blades. Maybe she wouldn't let him kiss her a third time! When she didn't turn away, he put his arms around her waist.

Still she said nothing! She was too frightened to talk—the same way she was frightened at the cypress tree shadows. Now they were out of the village, these shadows were falling across the road, stretching their tips on the opposite wall as if alive.

Abruptly, halfway down the path, she sat down on a rock, hiding her face in her hands on top of the shawl which had slipped from her head. Her hands were like iron, like the tines of a pitchfork.

Even if he couldn't figure out how to do it, Borio wanted to talk; he bent down close beside her. The Ghisola he had known for so long and had been with him a moment ago did not seem the same person sitting next to him now. She was squeezing her legs so tight they looked like an upside-down plow.

Holding her hands and struggling wordlessly, Borio was sorry already for what was happening; he took no pleasure in what he was doing. "Oh yes, . . .Oh yes you will . . ." he managed to say.

Their sweaty fingers were slipping together. He had an urge to
break them and they glared at each other as if ready to fight but by
now there was no turning back.

She loosened the grip on her legs. And then she burst into tears.

Since he was older, Borio was able to get her to do what he
wanted. He had a large bump on his head and no beard or moustache. He wore his hair close-cropped and low on his temples; his
eyebrows were like long black bristles that met on top of his nose.

By the next day Ghisola was already jealous and went to see
him.

His eyes were still moist, the hair on his tiny forehead even softer.

Borio had completely lost his head and was even ready to marry
her. But then the foreman got to her too and in spite and jealousy
they told everyone everything. At this the young men she had so far
kept at a distance refused to leave her alone.

If she was in the fields, they would go look for her under the fig
or pear trees; when she came back they would be waiting in the
junipers. To protect herself she would scratch and bite and then cry
and dash back up to the house. But afterwards the whole thing would
make her want to break out laughing and she wouldn't go to bed
until they had gone by under her window. One even tried to climb
her wall. And some would throw stones at the door.

The foreman was ready to take his shotgun to them, the way he
would with wild rabbits.

For her part, she was growing weary of the daily beatings she got
from her parents and ready to live on her own. So she found a job as
a lady's maid in Castellina, not too far from Radda.

After dipping way down to a small stream and mill, the Siena
road rises across the contorted and tangled lines of the hills, all of
which share the same gentle slope and appearance. The grape vines
are jumbled with stone retaining walls, cypress trees surround the
farm buildings, and in the distance there is a bell tower so far away
that it disappears at the first turn in the road. The road seems to
twist as though impatient with its own length and the more it bends,
the quieter it becomes and the drier and lonelier the countryside.

Some of the hills are flat, covered with stones and brush, maybe with a vine-pole cross lying on the ground alongside the shortcut that the peasants and their animals take.

There are also ragged oak groves with the dips and swells of other hills visible through the leaves, and steep slopes that level out suddenly and then drop down three or four times before they come out onto rolling fields, red clay terraces, or cliffs.

On the other side of Fonterutoli there is a village with just four shops arranged as though on a city streetcorner. Here the road gets steep and this is its highest point.

Sometimes there is a vista of a broad swatch of forest with a bird soaring over it and water gushing from an old beaten up downspout, the only one on the whole road, into a massive drinking trough below.

Forest silences that last for hours! A silence of boulders clasped in a tree roots' embrace. But when the wind sweeps down from peaks that are rapidly turning transparent, the terrifying moaning and clamor of the contorted branches. The tremor you can hear when a branch pulls in its leaves and then springs back as a soft, melodious noise echoes in the woods. Smaller branches shear off, leaves thrash the gravel, and birds hurry by as if borne on the wind.

When there are thunderstorms the oaks try to squeeze close to the ground. The clouds, as if watching, begin to coalesce so tightly that not even the wind seems able to budge them.

But whenever the oaks stand still, the clouds pass over.

Beyond the village the road toils up in sharp turns like a strip of white caught between two green rollers. All at once it is cut off by enormous rocks and tumbles straight down for almost a mile to where you can see Castellina.

The hills at this point are higher on the right and more and more flat on the left all the way to the Este valley with its villages like small heaps of stones. Then come the foothills of Montagnola and Montemaggio with other ranges beyond that look from up there like distant clouds.

You almost always run into a sheep flock up there, trotting through the clearings and disappearing into the woods on the other side—or rushing down the path single file as if diving, the weight of the first dragging the others with him.

And the red oxcarts and teams of oxen, the peasant passengers that squat on their heels for the ride!

A motor car, one of the first, draws everyone who can to come gape from their windows and doors, astonished to see it whiz by as if they weren't even there, then returning to work with a knowing glance. Such a rush!

Women whose children had been playing in the dirt in the middle of the road would shout and curse.

After squeezing ostentatiously against the wall, a well-to-do foreman would go and complain to his pals. He'd perch on a stool, his peeled walking stick between his knees and his crooked back propped against the pruning saws, buggy whips, and ropes that hang down outside of a shop where they also sell sulphur, brushes, and hob nails.

He would stay there as long as two hours, spitting from the corner of his mouth and getting a boy to buy his cigar so that he wouldn't have to move.

"People like that should be clapped in jail, don't you think? There was no such foolishness in our day."

Laughing, he would open his mouth so wide you could see the groove in the middle of his pointed tongue—its tip so sharp it looked whittled!

In the noon-time silence that the blazing sun made even deeper, he would take out his watch and wait for the bells to begin to ring.

"What time do you have?"

As soon as the bells would start to sway, everyone would stand up amazed—as though the walls themselves were starting to shift positions. All the shops would close down at the same time. People who lived out of town would start home for dinner, though first lingering a bit in the sun, like dogs who stop to wag their tails whenever they meet someone.

The light was still falling on the bell tower's upper half; it looked ready to burst into flame.

After the bells stopped tolling, another bell could be heard in the forest, pealing away all by itself, the sound it made blending with the sheep bells' clinking.

A girl who moves from a neighbouring village always brings with her the prejudices, sympathies, and distastes people have for that place. In Ghisola's case, moreover, there had been a great deal of gossip—and titillating gossip too.

The priest, egged on by his Radda counterpart, gave a good scolding to the lady who had hired her for a maid. Ghisola realized that this man was a potentially fanatic persecutor. Whenever he looked her way, she could see it in his strange, dirty-white complexion, in his mouth that twisted to one side, and his bulging near-sighted eyes. At such times she would just keep on walking, her chest stuck out even further and more provocatively till she looked like a duck wagging its beak in the air.

Now she hated Radda! It wasn't true. Borio would never have acted like that with another girl—with one of her sisters, for example!

In her mind's eye she could see the procession all over again. It amused her, in fact, to think back about it, identifying each person in the crowd of singers oblivious to her as they followed the raw, worm-eaten cross whose drops of paint red as real blood splashed to the ground and spattered their clogs! She could feel the procession marching dizzily into her eyeballs! The canopy was askew and the music echoed as if it was coming from the twists and hollows of the valley. The music seemed almost to be talking and the bells were pealing so loudly it seemed they would tear loose from their moorings.

Ghisola had hoped that people would pay less attention to her in Castellina; but nothing was different.

Everybody knew something about her and those who didn't just made it up.

The mayor had grown concerned, afraid it might cause a real scandal. Certain women are all right in the city, he would say, but not in small towns. Especially not in Castellina! Though he was fond of Ghisola too—even had his eye on her himself.

Of all those in Castellina, there wasn't a single man she could talk to. As soon as they started to get friendly, someone would find out and go and blab about it. So now there was no way for men to come up to her.

It was all great fun for the young sports, however, who all pretended she was theirs.

Deep down—and never mind what they said about her—the town's half-dozen young ladies were jealous of the stir she was making and the way men looked at her.

But it was getting to be too much for Ghisola and she decided to leave Castellina too. "What was she doing there anyway in that nest of gossips?"

So, thanks to some contacts she had, and with the help of a procuress, less than a month later she was fixed up with a crockery salesman who had left his wife and had been on the lookout for just such a girl. When he found out how willing and how much to his liking she was, he set her up in a little house in a place near Badia a Ripoli where everyone called him Signor Alberto.

When she sent them the address, Ghisola wrote her parents that she had found a new job.

When Pietro's exams rolled around and he went to see her, Ghisola was quite happy to be living like this.

He went up to the little door where the blue paint was faded and sun-blistered and rang the bell. The shiny porcelain plaque with the house number on it was gleaming in the light and the dark blue numbers were dancing and blurring.

He heard footsteps, then a woman's voice as the door opened. Breathing deeply, as if his breath had liquified and was clogging his nostrils, he rushed up the stairs.

"Is Ghisola here?"

The woman was curious and smiled at his embarrassment.

"I'll call her immediately," she answered—and it was as if the entire room had spoken.

He could sense the anger of his own first, unexpected reaction. Fixing his mind on nothing at all, he tried to remember her photograph and the emotion he had felt looking at it.

Shuffling her slippers, the woman went out. Alone now in the sudden silence, Pietro began to wish he were somewhere else. His feelings seemed at odds both with the place and with Ghisola. Was she really living here?

There was a slit in the mat over the window that let a ray of sun into the middle of the room where it glowed peacefully. But the silence seemed an abyss, an incomprehensible ambush! Nonetheless, he felt happy. He heard a patter of rapid footsteps: it was Ghisola!

Recognizing him, she laughed, blushing; then everything vanished except her smile. When he looked in her direction he was unable to make out her face and incapable even of saying hello.

She patted his hand and asked him to sit, then leaned back on the table waiting for him to start.

She was confused, even on the verge of tears. But she wanted him to notice how good-looking she was and got herself under control. The streak of light, which now was falling on her skirt, made everything brighter.

His own, wonderful Ghisola! He had found her again! "How long have you been here?" he managed to ask, getting up abruptly though with his eyes still turned to the wall.

She tossed back an answer he didn't like at all. Then, her hands clasped tight in front of her, she demanded, "Are you engaged to be married?"

"No."

For some strange reason he wanted to lie.

"You are too—I know you are."

Making a knowing gesture and looking amused, she kept right on talking. "Do you think I haven't had my eye on you?"

Pietro was so happy he was speechless.

She noticed this and began to look gentler in the eyes and the mouth. Even though Pietro had not been able to look at her, he figured it was time for him to say something. "I've thought about you the whole time."

When Ghisola turned toward the door, the strip of light followed the motions of her skirt, bouncing around as if trying to escape.

"Do you think that woman can hear us?" Pietro asked softly.

Ghisola had wondered about this. The idea amused her because of the fun they would have with it later, squeezing each other's arms they would be laughing so hard. "Maybe," she said finally, noticing his embarrassment and realizing she had to make some sort of answer. "It doesn't matter," she added.

"Who is she? What's she doing here with you?"

By now her lies were all used up. As if to say, "How nosey you are!" she stuck out her tongue. But then she answered, "She's a friend of the mistress."

"Does your mistress live alone?"

"All alone, with just this woman for company. No men are ever allowed in here."

"And do you like it? Does she treat you well? Do you have to work hard?"

"Oh, she likes me!"

"So now she's started to like her too," he mused, "the same way she used to like Giacco and Masa."

"Would you be in trouble if your mistress found me here?" he asked, alarmed and apprehensive. "Where is she?"

"She won't be back until late today. I'll have to tell her you came to see me."

"Go ahead and tell her. You won't get in any trouble. You mustn't tell lies," he said, trying to allude to their own relation. But the whole arrangement including the woman that Ghisola ignored left him astonished. He knew very well that she had to work to make a living. Something else had occurred to him: she might be insulted if he declared he was in love with her. After all, she used to be a peasant on his farm and might not even believe him. But his impatience got the better of him.

"What about you—have you thought about me at all?" he asked.

He could feel when he said this how tangled he was in his feelings and that he was trying to drag Ghisola there too. He had to get her away from these people he didn't even know and who seemed to be holding her prisoner.

All at once he fell silent, while she made one of those gestures that seems to reveal a whole life. Pietro, however, hadn't noticed. "Hasn't anyone ever fallen in love with you?" he asked anyway.

When she didn't answer, he repeated his question. Still she didn't answer. Now he felt that, for the first time, he had gone too far. Still, she was going to have to tell him the truth pretty soon. When he asked if he could keep on talking to her the same as always, the ambush-like silence that followed was so new to him he was delighted.

Her expression somewhere between good-natured and calculating, she was waiting for him to lift up his head. "Do you like me now?" she asked, as if joking.

He was too happy to be able to answer.

Nothing except the two of them and that room existed any-more.

"Could you still love me?" Ghisola continued.

"As long as you haven't been with someone else!" he answered, speaking with great difficulty and as though in someone else's voice.

The silence was so deep it seemed they could hear each other's joints moving in their bodies and each avoided the other's gaze.

It bothered him that she was a servant and might get in trouble with her mistress when she found out about his visit. Going over to the window, he pulled aside the green mat; there, in a dazzling pool of sunshine, were some bamboo plants in the middle of the flower gardens. In a single bound Ghisola rushed to his side and pulled him back.

"Don't look out there!"

He was terrified, as though the bricks were coming loose from the window because of his action. But he could feel his blood rush when Ghisola touched him. The same as before!

Quickly, she moved away. "It's true," she laughed, before he could get a grip on himself. "You are still in love with me."

Pietro could feel his head spinning as if from a narrow escape and joined in with Ghisola's laughter. She pretended not to believe him. "But not *just* with me!" she finished.

He couldn't think and his words tumbled out helter-skelter.

"Why do you answer that way? If I say that I am . . ."

Even their hands seemed to be talking. Ghisola suddenly seemed far in the distance, no longer part of an illusion, though he seemed to be struggling with a hostile presentiment that prevented his call-ing her to come to his side. His dream of love was still far off! What a deep dream it was!

He mustn't tell her how beautiful she was, for a compliment like that would seem suspect. Her beauty wouldn't be worth anything if it weren't for the sincerity so like his own that accompanied it.

He wanted her to know about this sincerity, to take pride in it. His moral convictions, inseparable in him from his feelings for re-demption and social justice, made this imperative. Above all, he had to set her an example. He promised that afterwards he would tell her everything.

But he couldn't think what more to say and seemed vaguely constrained to leave. He stood up stiffly, glanced at Ghisola from the middle of the room, put out his hand, and crept out the door—banging his shoulder on the jamb as he went.

Since her friend was due back any time, she was pleased the visit had come to an end so quickly.

The stairs were made of worn concave bricks; looking down, he could see his feet crashing right through them.

He was suddenly seized by a powerful trembling. Shutting the door with a crash that seemed enormous, he looked up to where Ghisola was on a narrow iron balcony nodding goodbye. But he was too weak to respond. He turned around twice, feeling tender toward her and hoping she would still be there. At the same time, he recognized that it was getting more difficult for him to wave back. He returned to the city in a daze.

Even though he was following the sidewalk along the embankment, he didn't look down once at the strip of greenish water streaked with blue that was the Arno. Some carts full of sand were waiting on a spit in the river and the water around them, shallower than elsewhere, flashed and glittered in the light.

The noise of the city sometimes seemed distant, fading and returning a moment later. Hurrying as he walked, Pietro kept forgetting where to turn and had to stop and go back.

When he arrived at the Archibusieri Embankment, the goldsmiths' shops on top of the Ponte Vecchio's twin pillars looked like a series of rolls with a single crust. The other buildings were clinging to the tops of the red wooden buttress-braces, their walls lacerated by windows that were too wide and too closely set together.

On the other side of the Arno the houses were dirty, gray, and old. They huddled together as if frightened of being torn down and looked like thin, multicolored strips pasted to other structures on the bridge: juxtaposed rectangles of different sizes made out of buildings and water.

The Arno washed against the buttresses. In the silence made by the river and buildings you could hear a distant rustling, sometimes in cadence with a tolling bell. The cypresses at Torre al Gallo stood sweet and still in the air.

This side of the Arno, the half-open shops were scorched by the sun; beneath their short awnings on the empty streets that led into the city the shade was too warm.

At San Miniato and on the Belvedere Hill, however, the trees made a high hedge among the scattered white villas on the other side of the Borgo San Jacopo roofs.

At Poggio dell'Incontro the hill was light blue and luminescent.

At the Ponte Vecchio the wind was flapping the goldsmiths' faded awnings and blowing the street dust into the river. At the end of the Santa Trinita bridge between the Cestello church and the apse of San Iacopo, snowy statues were casting yellow shadows next to the water. Then came the Santo Spirito bell tower and the lower, more widely spaced houses behind it that ran all the way to the Pignone chimneys. Then, isolated almost, the Carraia bridge and, in the distant light beyond, the first trees of the Cascine Park.

It was very late when he got home. He reorganized the books he had brought with him from Siena, and unpacked his laundry. He woke up two or three times in the night. "It won't be long to tomorrow!" he said loudly and happily before falling asleep each time.

For the entire morning, he couldn't decide what to do. But by evening he was sure that he was really in love with her; so he wrote her a letter. Even if he couldn't remember what Ghisola's face looked like, her gestures, which he could see only indistinctly, seemed to fill the air surrounding him. The color of her dress was a ray of light that flashed like lightning before him.

Ghisola had her friend read the letter. Since she was worried that Beatrice, the maid Pietro had seen with her, might say something, she had already given Signor Alberto her version of the visit.

"How come he's writing?" he asked with a laugh. "It seems he's been in love with you for a long time. What a strange letter. Let me read it again."

This time, after each sentence, he would stop and look at Ghisola where she was leaning on his shoulder.

They both recognized that these were feelings they would never experience and lived them vicariously through the letter. When he came to the end, Signor Alberto gave his mistress a kiss.

"He's completely crazy about you."

Taking the sheet of paper, she tore the letter to bits. Then, partly to make him laugh some more, partly because she was so happy, she started to to strut and twirl on her high-heeled shoes. "How can you be in love with someone like that?" he persisted, amused.

"It's easy," she said, twisting her body around.

"It seems that you don't tell me everything."

Then, taking her by the ear, he whispered, "Do you . . . with him too?"

"Certainly not," she snapped, straightening. "But if we were married, why then we'd have to, wouldn't we?"

He'd have to respect her if that were the case!

"I just want to make sure—for your own good—that he really loves you and really is rich—the kind you've dreamed of finding. Otherwise, I'd say you can stay where you are."

"If he's rich? His father owns ten farms and a huge restaurant."

"And what about his consent?"

"I bet he's the one who sent him here."

Signor Alberto believed Ghisola and was happy for her.

As she was getting the plates from the cupboard to set the table, she realized that she didn't have to give up her lover if she didn't want to.

But business was not going well and his placid, lazy life was about to come to an end. Ghisola would watch carefully when he nodded his head in dreams. She was sure he was about to make a decision he might not want to reveal.

"What's wrong with you tonight?" she would say, worried he had been thinking too much. "Is it your nerves again?"

"You're right about this," he answered smiling. "I really am too old for you and am going to have to give you up. I think you should get married."

"Why do you have to talk about it? Is it absolutely necessary for you to do that? You make me furious."

"You're the one who's been talking about it, Ghisola. However, I've got an idea."

"What?"

"You've got to arrange it in such a way that he'll think afterwards that he's made you pregnant! That shouldn't be too hard. What do you think?"

Her back to the light, she bit at her lip and and ran her finger on the edge of her plate.

"Well?" he asked.

"I don't even want to talk to him anymore. If he comes here again I'll throw a bucket of water on him."

And she rang the electric bell to tell Beatrice to bring the supper. "You'll be richer than I am," Signor Alberto exclaimed, as if this were the conclusion he had been striving to reach.

"Just don't bring him into my house," he added more seriously.

She turned and looked away guiltily.

". . . to have your fun."

But when she laughed it hurt his feelings.

"And I don't want anybody from Badia to see you together. Everyone knows me here."

"I'm losing her too," he went on to himself. "This is the way it had to end, I suppose." Attempting a smile, he smoothed back his moustache, started to look in her eyes, then pinched her hard.

"Understand?"

She had to laugh to keep from crying. But he refused to be moved. "Can't you even make him kiss you?" he asked in mock doubt.

"He's a lot smarter than I am," he added jokingly. "You could always do whatever you wanted with me."

This made them both laugh. Then, since the maid had just come in with their supper, they sat down to eat.

Ghisola was flattered at how much Pietro was in love with her. So, instead of answering by mail, she went to see him in person. Why was it really impossible for him to marry her? Then, when she went back to Siena, she could return as a lady instead of a peasant.

When she got there, Pietro was in his room with a book in his hand, flipping the pages instead of studying. He had one rather than two exams to take, but he couldn't concentrate on anything but Ghisola. There was no need for him to take the exam, absolutely not! He had to do what he was doing!

When she came through the door without even knocking, his heart gave a leap.

"Come in," he said. "I was expecting you."

Sitting down and pushing back the veil on her hat till it touched the imitation violets, she seemed quite serious.

"Take it off," he said.

He had never said a thing like that to a woman!

She smiled good-humoredly, as though she could tell or else suspect from his voice how new this was for him. After peering through the room with feigned suspicion, she went to the mirror and took the pin from her hat, sticking it in her mouth first and then putting it down next to the hat on the marble dresser.

How beautiful she was! If only he could marry her that very instant! They sat down face to face, he smiling in embarrassed joy and she careful to do the same. Their hands inched closer across the tabletop and he silently squeezed her fingers, one by one, as if to convince her there was nothing wrong in what they were doing.

The sun on the slats of the lowered blind were making it turn red.

As she half-closed her eyes, he got up and kissed her. But he wanted to scold her too, saying, "You can trust me—but what if I didn't really love you like this?" Terribly excited by the smell of her sweat and determined to prove he really did love her, he squeezed her hands tightly.

When she met his glance, Ghisola would lower her eyes, but always with a smile that seemed to ask that he understand and not take advantage of her inexperience by making love like that. Coughing, she leaned back in her chair again.

She was his then! How could he ever repay such bliss?

"Can you love me too?" he asked.

Head down, Ghisola said nothing. Gently, in a way he hoped she would appreciate, he tried to force her to answer. So now, for absolutely the first time, and making believe she didn't know how, she kissed him, scrubbing her mouth with her handkerchief afterwards as if sorry for what she had done. "I have to go home," she said.

"She shouldn't stay much longer," Pietro thought.

When he asked permission to kiss her again, Ghisola pretended she was angry that he hadn't asked the first time. This mortified him so deeply he didn't know what to say. The pupils in her eyes had turned the color of things under water.

But when she was putting her hat back on, she pricked herself on the finger. So she could hurt herself, even while he was standing there watching! Grabbing her hand, he watched the blood drop get bigger and bigger; just when it was going to fall, he sucked it into his mouth.

She was amused and happy to let him. And she smiled at him as if he were a little boy, sweetly and in a way that was already kinder and more intimate.

Pietro felt inebriated.

"I'll never forget this," he said.

In the Piazza Beccaria, where the trees were bending under the wind as if trying to wriggle back into the ground, she dropped her handkerchief. He picked it up and held it tight in his fist until it was time to say goodbye. The handkerchief was almost as important as her dress.

"When will you come back?"

Ghisola wasn't sure if her lover was really ready to let her do what she wanted.

"I don't know . . ."

Pietro was struggling to understand if this was supposed to make him angry or glad. It didn't seem possible that she was leaving.

"Tomorrow?"

Not knowing whether it would be a false step or not, he didn't insist.

"That's too soon. Five days from now," she smiled, trying to gain time.

"Remember that I'll be waiting . . . Don't you believe me? Say that you believe me."

"I know," she smiled again.

"Can I write to you? . . . But do you know how to read?"

"No."

Though she wanted to feel superior and was tempted to lie, she blushed instead and hung her head.

"And who will you get to read the letter? It will be a woman, won't it! . . . Mind that only a woman can read it to you."

"A woman, of course—I know that without your having to tell me."

She tugged with her hand at her lower lip as Pietro watched in ecstasy. "That woman I saw when I came to visit?" he asked, eager to believe she was not trying to lie.

But Ghisola could see what he was doing. "Someone else," she answered, laughing. "Don't ask anything more."

"Come back soon," he said.

All at once a thought came over him. "Why do I always do what she says? But how proud and happy I feel when I do it!"

She went off without once turning back. He watched her disappear around a bend where a cypress towered over a garden wall. She seemed a stranger who was ignorant of their love, though his feelings for her were even more real than she was herself.

In the park, a leaf from a tree brushed against his face. At Poggio a' Meli he would have ripped it away.

Pietro waited for her every single day. He could still see her sitting there with her arms on the table. But he had a growing feeling that he had only started to know her and didn't yet love her. Though they were on his mind constantly, he didn't take his exams, imagining as though in a terrifying hallucination that when he was interrogated he couldn't answer.

Instead, so impatient it almost drove him to tears, he went to see Ghisola.

"Were you expecting me?" he asked when she came to the door. He was surprised to realize that he really was in love with her.

But she insisted he keep his distance. "Maybe," she answered.

Though he found it distressing even to talk, he heard himself saying, "Couldn't we just walk down the road together? Are you alone?"

Ghisola thought a minute. Then she answered, "Meet me in front of the Badia church."

Pietro had the uncomfortable sense that a vague lie was hanging over him. It was only because he had suggested it that he decided to wait for her.

Although it was windy, the July sun was burning down everywhere. At the curve in the road that led to Bisarno the cypress trees were swaying and the light seemed to move in tune with the wind. Some branches from an olive tree were sticking out over a wall and flailing it with their tender green leaves. Even their shadows seemed made out of leaves and were hardly distinguishable from the real ones.

Taking short steps, she came toward him. She had no hat on and wore a small gold locket on a chain round her neck.

When Pietro explained he had to go back to Siena, he was afraid he was going to appear ridiculous. But after walking silently beside him while he kept staring at her hands, she asked, "When are you leaving?"

"Tomorrow."

"Then we won't be seeing each other again."

The half-mocking calm of her answer surprised him. "Will you always think of me?" he asked with a sigh.

"Always," Ghisola answered firmly, almost obediently.

"You must think I don't love you very much," she went on, seeing at a glance how unhappy he was.

"I trust you," he answered, not caring it if was the truth.

Ghisola, head down, smiled again. But this time she let the pleasant expression linger on her face for a while.

Silently, the wind was lifting white dust clouds in the street and it seemed too lonely for anyone to have ever walked down it. Ghisola seemed plumper, beautiful in a different kind of way. "Yes, even dressed like this she still looks wonderful." But he couldn't keep his eyes away from her locket, wanting to remove it and worried that people would stare even more at her chest if he didn't.

Ghisola had noticed this and was waiting expectantly.

"Why do you wear that?" he asked when he noticed this.

She blushed as if she were trying to protect the locket.

"Did you buy it, or get it as a present?"

"Someone gave it to me."

"Tell me who it was. Tell me right now."

He had stopped and was blocking her way.

"My sister Lucia."

"How long ago?"

"A year. When she came to see me."

"Does she like you?"

"She does, but I don't like her."

"Why not?"

"I don't know."

"Why? Tell me. You must tell me."

"I don't know. We have different kinds of character."

He could see that this might be true since they were completely different in appearance too—and he felt glad. But he was still jealous of her sister.

"I'll buy one for you and then you can wear mine," he said. "I mean you can wear yours because from now on what's mine is yours. What do you think of that?"

She felt like laughing, in fact, though this was certainly no time for that. Instead, saying nothing, she turned away. And since she had begun to walk quickly, as if in a hurry to get somewhere, he asked, "Is that woman expecting you?"

"Yes, we haven't been very careful."

"How can you say that when I love you so? You shouldn't worry about things like that."

Lengthening her step, she smiled without answering.

Pietro let her go on into the square, walking around it afterwards making believe he was expecting someone. But there wasn't anyone else there! He did see a dog with a huge arched hump go running by.

On the Grassina road he saw a hill that was a faded pale green and covered with olive groves mixed with slender cypresses.

When a tram came around the corner, he jumped on. The next time he looked, he was back in Florence past the Barriera on the glistening Lungarno; he could see all the bell towers in a single glance.

Thinking hard about it, Pietro had reached certain conclusions. "Even if she was caught between virtue and starvation, I still couldn't take advantage of her. I'd start to cry. I'd help her reform. Someone would come to respect and marry her. If that had happened, she would certainly have told me. Why wouldn't she tell me?"

By now, on the contrary, she was taking on an air of extraordinary purity. He was jealous and started to cry. "She has to be mine! I want to love her! Why shouldn't I?" Wasn't it his moral duty as well? But could he arrange for a better life than what he had at his father's house?

"Your father's rich," Ghisola had told him, "and everything depends on what he thinks. And he certainly won't be in favor."

When Pietro came back from Florence and told him he loved Ghisola and wanted to marry her if he would gave his permission, Domenico didn't even answer. But he felt as angry and cornered as a mother fox whose den has been set to the torch.

Neither one of them said a word about the exams. Pietro didn't want his father to know what had happened and Domenico was trying not even to think about it, though it made him want to take him and throw him against the wall like a pillow.

When Pietro came back from the long, lonely walks he took in the country, walks when he seemed to be asking the very air for advice, he couldn't believe that Ghisola had ever loved anyone but him. A thing like that would have ruined her beauty. He was just jealous!

"Is this really Siena?" he would sometimes ask. "It doesn't seem like Siena. The sky is too blue—not at all the way it used to be." In Piazza del Campo he noticed a pale tepid light that on summer afternoons lingered into the evening. The inside of the square seemed illuminated as if by a lantern and the mysterious, silent people moving across it seemed to belong to a faraway time.

"Once Ghisola is here, I'll be able to explain how I feel."

Each morning he woke up with a sigh. How vividly he remembered his dreams!

But life was impossible without Ghisola. It was the middle of August when he decided she should wait in Radda until they were married. It would only be for a year, eighteen months at the most. After all, why shouldn't he get permission? He would rest easier once she was at Radda.

He got the cash for the trip from Rebecca.

But the first few hours he spent in Florence he felt as though he were back in Siena, up on the Via Camporegio where he went every day on his way to the technical school. It is not a long distance from the rough, reddish mass of San Domenico down to the jumble of buildings that butt up to the Duomo, but when you look down at the huge abyss of Fortebranda it takes your breath completely away.

The hospital looming above the city walls was turning from blood red to burnt umber as the sky's deep blue gave way to gray. The earliest stars were twinkling in a pattern that drove him almost wild with anguish.

The narrow alleys that looked like splits or fissures were changing to black.

Among the gardens and terraced orchard, each enclosed by a squared, often communal wall, and out along the dips, swells, and varying slopes of the hills, the glow of the night seemed to descend like a heavy rain.

A drunk started to sing and then stopped. Toiling up crookedly toward the buildings, the Costaccia was like the edge of an abyss. The sheer drop of the Costone was steadied by a thick, heavy arch that permitted another street to cross on top of it.

No two roofs, not even adjacent ones, were quite the same height. Large and small clumps of houses fell into crooked, rough parallels that in two or three places interlocked into corners. Then they would circle, knot, and entwine, mixing and tangling into squashed or broken curves, then change abruptly according to the shape and slopes of the hills, the turns of the streets, and the squares that looked like holes when seen from above.

Suddenly there was a space between two buildings while the others kept clutching, jostling, and shoving, then climbing again and veering quickly behind still more structures rushing in confusion from the opposite side. Now these new ones are the highest, but only to be interrupted and pushed down into a broader, irregular circle that is flat but twisted and jammed with structures that push and shove crookedly, sideways, as best they can, and are elbowed aside by others that all seem selfishly struggling to achieve a more comfortable position.

At Porta Ovile, Fortebranda, and Tufi, the houses are so low they seem to be trying to sink into the fields. Others are piled on top of them and thus restrained from their headlong rush to disperse. The highest points of the city are like signal markers that the buildings must obey or risk being left on their own.

Seen from on high, the city is a confused maelstrom of buildings smashing like landslides into each other. Sometimes, to the contrary, there are as many as ten long roofs that lie perpendicular to still others beyond.

Above this confusion, the Mangia bell tower stands serene.

The olive and cypress trees seem reluctant to leave the city, now that they have come in from the country, and make themselves places among the houses outside the walls.

But no matter how reassured he was by Giotto's bell tower, Santa Maria dei Fiori, the well-known streets he had often walked, he could sense his father coming after him and an increasingly frenzied desperation took control of him. He longed to talk to a schoolmate again, to straighten out the misunderstanding, and to explain that there was a secret reason he couldn't reveal that had caused him to fail. Much as he disliked secrets, he could feel an intense need for something to hide, something perhaps the same as his soul.

A lemon seller sat underneath a green, wooden-ribbed umbrella at the entrance to the Ponte alle Grazie. A porter and someone indistinct were leaning dozing against the embankment wall.

Out of the trees at San Miniato a lark flew like a glittering object in the direction of the Cascine Park.

Nearer the Piazza della Signoria, cooler now that it had been sprinkled with water, people began to reappear. In the Via Calzaioli and the Duomo square it was even more crowded. The hill of Fiesole rose green at the end of the Via Cavour.

Though the tram was empty, Pietro blushed when he got off at Badia. He checked beneath the blinds of the houses to see if a face was peering out. There was nothing but dusty geranium plants.

Though Ghisola opened the door, she didn't invite him inside. He started to scold her for not having gone to Radda and she explained that she had been waiting for him and had to be certain her parents would take her back.

He couldn't understand why he had the feeling he had already been with her for a long time.

"Why shouldn't they take you back? Are they mean to you?"

"I don't like living there."

He noticed that she had answered in just that way and no other.

"You mustn't say no," he pleaded, stroking her face. "You have to wait at home. That's what I want."

"Why am I asking her this?" he wondered.

"If that's what you want . . ."

Now it was clear she would do what he wanted, he added, "Come to Siena."

She smiled and motioned for him to be silent.

It seemed to him that she ought to enjoy doing what she was told. But Ghisola was tempted to take it all as a joke. "Don't you like me any more?" she asked.

"Why shouldn't I?"

And he ran his hands over her face. She stared at his fingertips, then moved away.

"Why not come now? I'll wait for you in the road next to the Badia."

"I will. Go on now."

He took her hands in his and kissed them but she pulled away and nearly shut the door on him.

"She hasn't had a happy life," he thought as he left, "and isn't happy now to live in a house that isn't hers. Maybe her parents don't write any more. As for her relatives, they're jealous. She seemed even more passionate than ever before, though I still have to respect her—now more than ever. I'd hate her afterwards if I didn't respect her."

He never asked himself, on the other hand, how she could go off with him the moment he asked.

Signor Alberto had become involved in a bankruptcy suit; for two weeks no one, not even Ghisola, had seen him. He spent almost all his time at the office or with one of those lawyers where Ghisola used to pay him brief visits. He advised her to go back to Radda, at least until after the trial. In this way, his wife's parents, who were testifying, wouldn't make his case any worse.

He no longer gave her any money and often Ghisola was reduced to nothing but bread and fruit. But she refused to go home and since there was no place else she could go, she was biding her time before deciding anything.

When Pietro arrived, all she had to do was ask Beatrice to tell her friend goodbye and not to forget her.

Even so, Beatrice—whose employer had clearly left her instructions—had to remind her several times that Pietro was waiting.

When she hugged her goodbye, the woman was crying so tenderly that Ghisola began to smile through her tears.

Pietro was waiting near the door, hoping every step he heard was Ghisola's. Finally he saw her.

A kind of hostile respect lay between them and neither uttered a word. While he was trying to meet her eyes, she kept looking around, avoiding his gaze though she could see everything. They could feel their reserves lessen, however, once they were forced to exchange a few words.

When a tram stopped they got on.

Her straw hat had a single, black velvet ribbon and a light veil she wore over her face; her gloves were white knit. This coarse elegance moved Pietro so deeply he gave her a pat on the hand. Once they were married, she would certainly dress better. Even so, everyone was staring and this made him happy.

Since there was not much time before their train, they rushed straight to the station from the Duomo square. The crowds in the street brought them back to themselves and their decision, and now they did look into each other's eyes. Though they scarcely exchanged a word doing it, they got on the train for Siena. It was only when their compartment began to empty that he asked, "Why don't you lift your veil?"

"Then I can to see you better," he added in a whisper.

After she did what he asked, they took their old places across from one another.

"If you want to relax, I'll come sit next to you. Do you want to put your head on my shoulder?"

"It doesn't matter."

The glances they exchanged seemed to link them together the same way their souls did—souls that now felt heavy within them.

The countryside was streaming by, escaping much too rapidly! It seemed to Pietro that it was trying to get away from him, refusing to understand, and in the end disapproving. This was one more reason he had to love Ghisola.

Like his excitement, the day too was beginning to fade. In the bright morning sunlight, the railway cars seemed about to catch fire and burst into flame. At the stations they were passing the cars seemed frightened of being abandoned on side tracks that lay in a jumble of straight and curved rails that glistened with a sad, dead light that they carried with them into the darkness and mist of the distance. Though completely divorced from him, the country kept changing according to his mood.

A train pulling out from Poggibonsi became so foreshortened that you couldn't tell if the end of the last car was stopped or still moving: just like some of his illusions. Other cars were being switched back and forth, their wheels revolving in the same direction as they rolled one by one down identical tracks. He was brought to the brink of tears by the sight of a freight train whose patient, sealed cars were painted red with white numbers. He could feel them in his soul twisting and crushing.

Alone and abandoned, he had forgotten all about Ghisola. She was sitting looking with intense curiosity, her eyes fixed in what he thought was an intriguing stillness.

Seeing her watching, he gave a sigh. "You like me better today, don't you!" he exclaimed.

She looked back in digust, then lowered her eyelids to conceal her expression; her soul itself seemed to be slipping away.

Pietro hadn't noticed and was waiting for her to say something.

Ghisola made him sit down and they took each other by the hand.

The passengers getting on and off and the signals exchanged at the stations only augmented her sense of tedium.

When they got to Siena she refused to go to her aunt's.

"Why don't you want to go?"

"She'll want to know everything. I'm not telling anybody about my life."

She could live any way that she pleased!

He could sense how free and independent she was. "That isn't nice: she's your aunt," he said, trying to be sure she had nothing to hide.

"What if I went to a hotel?"

"It wouldn't be right if you went by yourself."

"But you know, don't you, that I belong completely to you?"

She was getting insistent, hitting his arm with her fan and adopting the tone and gestures of a child. "Oh come on," she said; "let me. You always do what you want to do. Won't you let your Ghisola do what she wants for one night?"

They had almost arrived at the restaurant and it was already getting dark, so they had to decide quickly.

Beyond the San Francesco basilica they could see clouds hanging in a low line like fire.

When a passerby paused to look them over, they quickened their pace.

Suddenly, on the left, they could see the church of the Madonna di Provenzano and part of Siena. The buildings seemed crowded much too closely together.

Without noticing, they had both stopped talking. Via Vallerozzi seemed stairs of broad roofs all the way down to old fort Salimbeni where the black shadow of an enormous fir tree stretched across the buttress. The top of the Tower was somewhere beyond the fort. Still further—imprisoned almost by another esplanade of buildings—was the dome of the Madonna di Provenzano. The roofs of the three streets that knot together at Porta Ovile were descending once more, the buildings bending to the side as though they couldn't stand straight. A certain stretch of one of these streets looked like a stone mill race that had captured a woman who had momentarily stopped there.

The pointed roofs kept flattening down until they reached the last, lowest one that supported the remaining buildings.

Breaking out of his trance, Pietro took her hand and shook it. "I'm sorry I won't let you . . ." he went on. "But please listen."

Irritated, she stopped once again.

"Listen. I've been thinking about taking you to my father's for supper. I told him I was going to see a friend in Poggibonsi and I'll pretend we met on the train."

She hesitated before answering, waiting for a man who was watching to move on. "Will he believe us?"

The passerby's curiosity was starting to annoy them, to rattle their nerves.

"Of course he will!"

Head down, Ghisola stood there for some time. It wasn't that she needed more time to think, but rather that she didn't want her mind to wander.

"I don't much like this," she added.

Sensing they were on the brink of a quarrel, neither said anything more. The silence that followed was the kind that magnifies the slightest sound. Taking her arm, he led her to the door of the restaurant.

When he saw them arrive, Domenico did not come over, though he did wave at Ghisola and was almost ready to believe Pietro's tale. Pietro, for that matter, had never lied to him even once.

Rebecca's husband was going by, plate in hand. He stopped and announced, "As soon as I've served these people, I'll tell your aunt."

Ghisola thanked him, for she could tell that her relative might be an excuse for her presence in Siena.

Domenico was in a good mood. When he saw the smile on Ghisola's face, he could tell how different she was from when she lived at Poggio a' Meli. Although in the kitchen he put in their order as if she and Pietro were ordinary customers, he made it clear from the beginning: "These two won't have to pay."

Ghisola was not at all embarrassed and began to laugh. It was just pride that made her miserable when Domenico put her in her place. But Pietro made her furious. He had no sense and didn't count for anything even in his own house!

She refused to sit at the table, making it clear that she didn't need a restaurant to get something to eat. Pietro whispered not to cause a scene, promising that they would straighten everything out in the morning.

Hands in his pockets and head down, Domenico had been ignoring them as he rushed between the kitchen and where they were sitting. He went out to blow off some steam with his friend the grocer. Though when you were young it was all right to have fun, a son shouldn't bring his girlfriends home. But the grocer laughed at his rage, saying he should go on and have a good time since the girl involved was so pretty.

Ghisola didn't seem to have much appetite and hardly lifted her head from her food. But Pietro rubbed his feet against hers and kept trying to tease her out of her mood. When he left the restaurant, she was in the semidarkness next to the cupboard chattering with cousin Rosaura. Then Ghisola and the cousin went to see her aunt and told her a whole string of complicated lies, all with the most innocent air in the world.

"I can't permit you to sleep here tonight," said Rebecca. "But if the master doesn't mind, you can sleep with your cousin."

Curious to see what was going to happen, Ghisola came downstairs and went into the restaurant.

By now it was nearly midnight and all the tables had been cleared. The cooks leaned drowsily against the chopping block and the fire in the stove was dying as though the embers themselves were falling to sleep. The lights had all been lowered and the building was filled with the disgusting smell of different foods jumbled together.

Next to the sink there was a basket of fruit peels and leftovers.

Suddenly the night grew darker and for a few brief moments it rained. It was the sort of shower that immediately increases everyone's irritation the same way it makes the compost bubble from its heap in the center of the field.

Ghisola was sleepy and exhausted and the rain seemed to pour straight down on her soul, though without cleansing it. Even so, she felt stifled.

In the clouds lightning glittered noiselessly.

She knew she would feel this rain in her dreams. She tried to ignore it by paying close attention to everything they were doing and saying.

"Go and lock up," ordered Domenico, waking up from the sofa where he often snoozed a few hours before going to bed.

It was clear that something was bothering him—so much so that Rosaura hesitated for a moment. "I'm going to the house to get Ghisola sheets," she announced.

Domenico said neither yes nor no, turning away when Ghisola said goodnight and pushed provocatively by him.

The ceiling in Rosaura's bedroom was so low you could reach the beams from the bed. The wall was more than three feet thick with a narrow window that looked out on a tiny courtyard that winter or summer was always damp.

When Rosaura put down the sheets, Ghisola took off her jacket. "Where does Pietro sleep?" she asked

"In the same room he had as a boy. Are you going to go see him? How chubby your arms are!"

"Just feel how plump I've become!"

She had Rosaura pinch her on the thigh and then went out of the room.

She remembered the house distinctly and could move by feel nearly all the way from the entrance hall to the living room; there, because of the street light, it was less dark.

Since Domenico needed to pass through Pietro's room to get to his own, the door to Pietro's bedroom was open. She could see the table with its books and the mirror shining over the dresser. She went over to where the bed had been pushed to the wall and Pietro had fallen asleep.

When she bent and kissed him on the mouth, he did not wake up. "Ghisola!" he cried, shuddering in his sleep. "It's you."

Pietro couldn't understand why Ghisola had gotten it into her head to dislike her relatives. He complained to Rebecca, suggesting that she give her a talk.

"At least she should learn how to read," he added. "She promised she would."

But Ghisola knew how to divert attention.

He assumed that Domenico, the restaurant, and everything else must somehow have offended her and that she wanted to leave as soon as she could.

"What makes you think I want to live with your father, even if he lets me?" she said the next day.

Pietro knew he could promise nothing.

"When he's as sure as I am that all they've said is untrue, he'll respect you," he explained. "Why shouldn't he respect you? Why shouldn't he let you become my wife?"

But when he took her arm she knew it was impossible. "He hates me," she said. "And he doesn't want us to be in love. Don't forget how at Poggio a' Meli he sent me away when he found out about us!"

His plans, once so serious, were becoming ridiculous, each one more than the last. Pietro knew he had to let her go where she wanted. How sorry he was he had brought her to Radda! He didn't dare take her arm any more.

Ghisola knew she wasn't going to stay more than a few days; she didn't take any of it seriously, making sure at the outset that Domenico knew that she was leaving. With Pietro accompanying her, she went to her grandparents' at Poggio a' Meli, never once setting foot in the restaurant again.

A beautiful white tapestry, radiant with fireflies, hung on the olive trees while lightning flashes came and went like a liquid but dense light above the black Chianti hills.

Ghisola was sitting alone on the farmyard wall. That Masa and the others were out in the moonlight only deepened her rage. The moonlight appeared to stick to their clothes and they seemed to drag it with them wherever they went. She wanted to keep her distance from them, to make them forget she was even alive. They were nasty, disgusting women just like she used to be!

Trembling convulsively, she stretched out on the wall, staring at a star that was the biggest of all and seemed to be circling, jumping around, tugging at her temples with its every move.

Frightened she was about to loose her sanity, she shook her head and rubbed at her eyes.

When the women went in, she sat up and stared at their doors. The yard lay half in shadow all the way to the well and so did the arch where they kept the wagon. The shadows seemed shadows of other shadows.

The wall was the same one where she had once sat with a friend, trapping flies on their knees. How they would laugh when someone went by on the road!

The well frightened her; it seemed to be dragging the moon and her too down deep into its water. When she saw that her face was covered with moonlight, she hid it in her hands and then sat quietly.

After a little, she could hear someone walking across the farmyard—someone in bare feet. But she didn't budge, foolishly imagining she wasn't able. So Carlo sat beside her, coughed, and then cupped his hand on her breast. Lifting her face, she laughed blankly and dashed into the house.

Oblivious to the girl, Carlo had seen only her laugh.

Just then Pietro appeared in the open gate. Before going to Giacco's, he stopped to look at the moon that seemed to have just come out from the windows back of the house.

He was thinking how impressed the farmhands would be when they heard he was in love with a peasant, someone just like them.

Pietro and Ghisola were taking the road that led from the farm-yard to the fields. They headed toward that same cherry tree where they had been together many years earlier; the memory of those moments seemed to hang from its branches.

Ghisola was jumpy and ready to give herself to him. "Can't you see what's happening?" she almost said. But Pietro was caught in a deepening ecstasy and seemed to be walking in his sleep.

"Why don't you pay any attention to me?" he demanded.

In fact, she was turning to him only now and then and would have been glad to leave him there. Controlling her nerves as she had on the wall, and imitating his voice to herself, she halted and looked at the sky.

He trusted her perfectly. "We'll never see another night like this," he exclaimed. "I can see the stars shining even in your eyes!"

He gave her a long kiss. She pulled her head back and moved away. Was he crazy? When he didn't let her pull back again, she cried out with joy. Ghisola was beside herself with desire, like a flawed jug that finally splits open at the seam.

"If only you were more of a man!" she couldn't help saying.

"I love you!" said Pietro, as if to himself.

Since the euphoria that had him in its grip was increasingly sensual for him too, he decided that they should go back. Ghisola must never know!

Masa was waiting at the rise in the road, arms on her hips and extremely distressed by the lewd comments made by the farmhands back in the yard. Giacco went into the house, worried at how long they had left the oil lamp burning. There was a moth with a body as thick as a man's finger that kept bumping into it; the flutter of its wings made him look up to where the door was half-open.

When they got back to the yard, Pietro and Ghisola were less tightly embraced. "Don't go out any further," Masa said in an undertone.

The hands, partly out of regard for the young master, were careful not to say anything. In the moonlight, their faces were clearly visible and seemed completely smooth and without wrinkles.

The pole for the straw stack was tilting crookedly toward a lime tree.

How wonderful it was at Poggio a' Meli!

Once through the gate, they started to hold hands again. In the pale branches of the olive trees the countless fireflies that sometimes stuck gummily to their hands seemed to be growing in number.

Hidden in the shadow behind the hedge, they started to kiss. She was leaning on the wooden gate while he pressed against her. But Pietro suddenly realized that she was rubbing her thighs too passionately and he broke away and gave her a scolding.

Masa was more and more upset at what was happening, especially after she heard what the hands were saying in the farmyard; she had to stuff her mouth with her fist to keep from answering. She called out to them just as Pietro began to scold Ghisola, and so the two of them came back inside.

One of the hands was scratching furiously at his head trying to control his hilarity. Bent over and with his hands on his knees, Carlo snickered each time he saw Masa; in the palm of his hand he could still feel the impression of what he had touched.

The gossip this created lasted more than a month.

Carlo peered out his door for some time, waiting to see when they left. There was no way he could go to bed without saying something to Ghisola.

In order not to be on the road alone coming home, Ghisola asked the daughter of one of the hands to go back to the village with her and Pietro.

They walked arm in arm, the other girl careful to keep her distance. When they turned, they could see her smiling, attentively and excitedly at first, then almost frantically.

They kissed some more before they parted. At this, the girl, who had been peeking through her fingers clasped over her face, flung herself down in the center of the road and began to roll in the dust.

"Oh my," she cried, as if no one else were there. "Oh my, oh my, what am I doing here!"

"Get dressed."

He had caught her unawares, arms bare in the bedroom. He wanted to kiss her and was trying to make her hurry and put her pink jacket back on.

"I like it better when you're dressed," he said. "You know very well that I couldn't kiss you otherwise!"

She was getting ready for the stagecoach back to Radda.

Things were still the same as before. Keeping himself carefully under control, Domenico was pretending to ignore Pietro and Ghisola, certain that time was on his side, and aware that the insinuating rumors had not been scotched. Pietro, for his part, still hadn't figured out how to hurry the wedding.

Masa kept going in and out, one eye on them and the other on the yard to see if the hands were hanging around watching. For her master's sake, she feared their tongues more than ever and could hardly wait for Ghisola to leave.

Masa didn't feel she deserved to have her granddaughter become Pietro's wife. Never, ever, had she expected such a thing! Why, she didn't dare even thank God for it for fear He would punish her for being so happy—though she also wanted to be certain first!

"You can't ask God for what you don't deserve," she would repeat.

Handing her the comb, Pietro buttoned Ghisola's jacket on the shoulder. When he reached the final button, she turned and they kissed some more.

Since they still had plenty of time, she lay down on the bed that was hers when she was a girl. The look on her face was so stern it seemed sinister and anxious. She pushed Pietro's caresses away, refused to let him kiss her, and, no matter what he was trying to say, wouldn't answer. Her eyes were frowning and gloomy and her mouth was swollen with anger.

"What's wrong?" said Masa. "Don't you feel good?"

She snapped back her head as though her neck had gone stiff. Pietro took her hands.

"It's nothing. It'll pass in a minute. Though, is there something the matter with you? Leave her alone, Masa."

Ghisola looked at them—first one, then the other. When Pietro kissed her feet, she hid them under her skirt. Was it simply that she didn't like leaving? But this was no different from all the other times—times when just touching something that was hers: a pin, even her silver bracelet—had been enough to put her back in good humor. This was why he couldn't understand how she was willing to swap trinkets with people!

Ghisola didn't ever want to move again; she was thinking how she ought to stay there indefinitely, maybe forever.

Pietro and Masa hovering around her like that were giving her the shudders. How she'd like to give them a kick!

When Pietro finally convinced her to get up, pointing out that otherwise they were going to miss the stagecoach, she again felt an immense urge to say something nice and grimaced in a way that was both cruel and graceful.

By the time they arrived at the stagecoach stop, she had calmed down. She bent her legs as she walked, hitting her parasol on her knee at each step. She seemed like a child when she leaned against Masa and Pietro.

Masa was thinking about the farmhands and the unlocked house, and she kept turning and pursing her lips.

The stage was late. Before she left, the old woman crossed her stomach with her hands. "Let's hope everything works out!" she declared.

But Ghisola, moving further away from Pietro, who was staring at her intently, didn't even say goodbye.

The windows of Palazzo dei Diavoli were completely empty. On the way to the stagecoach stop they had passed a peasant's yard that was filled with heaped sheaves of grain; the sunlight seemed to rain in streams from the roof of the house and then bounce back up in a ring of flame.

From where they were now, they could see the walled trees of Vico Bello high on a hill that was green with fodder corn. Its olive trees seemed colorless or transparent and their shadows made the grapevine stalks look even thicker.

A beggar sat on the Cappella steps, sharing the same shade with them. They each pointed him out to the other, then smiled at hav-

ing had the identical idea. Then they waited to see him start gnawing at the bread he held clutched in his hands.

The coach arrived. A woman was in it alongside a drawn and
unshaven peasant, a convalescent going home with his wife from
the hospital. There was a red handkerchief next to him that was
filled with different kinds of medicine and his wife had a gray shawl
in her lap that she used in the evening to cover him up. The man's
eyes were glassy and he seemed uncomfortable, as though he hadn't
wanted the coach to stop and was expecting some trouble.

The side-curtains, lowered against the sun, were flapping.

The horse stopped with a jerk, his hind legs buckling. He was a
long and skinny nag—the kind with a high forehead and enormous
jaws. Whenever he breathed, his ribs stuck out between the brass
bossing of his trappings. Under the bit, there was an oats stalk caught
in his wrinkled lips. He stank of sweat and leaned to one side in the
shafts.

Pietro opened the carriage door with the stencil of the postal
insignia on it. Head down, Ghisola got in. When she indicated that
she wanted a kiss, Pietro kissed her, though he wished he could tell
her, "It's not right here!" As the coach began to move, she smiled at
him as if to herself.

After glancing at the couple as if she had just noticed them across
from her, she bowed her head and went suddenly pale. She had felt
something moving in her womb.

Hopelessly, and gripped by such anxiety it almost killed him,
Pietro was waiting for her to look back.

It was nearly September when he went to see her at Radda.

The town is a jumble of houses on the top of a small hill that is
visible from the woods several miles away. It is so quiet that from
out in the road you can hear people talking in their houses.

Pietro got a lift to Castellina in the buggy of a friend who agreed
to wait and take him back in the evening.

The rest of the way to Radda he went on foot. Crossing through
the woods, he could sometimes smell the odor of a flock of sheep
lingering among the oaks, boulders, and juniper bushes.

Beyond three cypress trees with slender blasted trunks that stood on the edge of an old abandoned road, was a roadside shrine once painted blue. The tumble-down wall leading away and a huge nearby hawthorn were both covered with ivy.

Beautiful forests covered the adjoining hills; the further he went, the thicker and denser they got though they were so light in color they seemed almost transparent.

Soon he arrived at Poggiarofani, a place where shepherds often stopped and where the road, which is very twisted, with hairpin turns and sharp switchbacks, reaches its highest point. Here you are halfway between the Arezzo Appenines and Santa Fiora mountain, though so far from both that the mountains, like the horizon, seem made out of air.

In the yawning valleys on both sides of the road, some birds flew by, heeling at first as if unsure which way to go, then disappearing into the depths again.

When he got to the town he was out of sorts and tired. By now his excitement was beginning to wane, and various doubts had begun to assail him. He was sure his father was going to be awful and everyone would think he had gone to see Ghisola because they were making love.

Just past the first houses he had to get out of the way of a passing carriage that was covered with white dust.

He met a woman and asked about Ghisola. She kept her eyes on him from the moment she saw him as her pitcher under the fountain spigot ran over with water.

She was staying, it turned out, with Lucia: her elder, married sister. He discovered which was her door and, finding it open, marched in and then out so that he could knock.

Three other women, curious to learn who he was, had already gathered in the narrow alley. Anxious to avoid their stares, he went back in the house without an answer.

Lucia, who had met him once at Poggio a' Meli, came to the landing to meet him. "Where's Ghisola?" he demanded without so much as a hello.

If Lucia hadn't been her sister, he would have been even more enraged that he hadn't been told sooner where she was. Her sister should realize how much he loved her.

"Upstairs," Lucia answered, seeing him overwrought.

"Call her," he said angrily. "No, don't. I'll call her myself."

But Ghisola had heard and came downstairs.

She seemed to have grown tanner in the few days of her absence, though the torn skirt she was wearing hung down to the floor.

Lucia left them standing there staring and went into the kitchen to make something to eat.

"Why aren't you at your parents' house?"

She looked at him blankly. "Do you still love me?" she asked, astonished.

This upset him. "Why do you want to know that?" he said. "Why shouldn't I love you?"

And he started to twist her wrist. Eyes on the floor, she let him do what he wanted without trying to stop him.

"You shouldn't wear that dress . . . What if someone saw you in it?"

"Well, what if they did then?" he insisted, curious to hear her answer.

Ghisola sulked and said nothing and Pietro regretted the remark: the same way you do after beating an animal and then finding out there was no reason for it.

"Your legs are showing . . . and the skirt is torn too."

He had not meant to say this at all and he felt on the brink of tears. Wanting to avoid physical temptation, he took her arm and pushed her into the bedroom. When Ghisola tried to pull away, the rest of the dress tore open and he saw her thigh. She blushed. He pulled her close and hid her face so she wouldn't be embarrassed for him!

"I didn't mean to, but I did see you."

Though Ghisola was prepared to take all her clothes off, she pulled the skirt back together. "Let me be," she said.

"Why do you dress like that?" Pietro asked, sorry now he had hugged her that way.

"I dress as I please. What are you doing out here at Radda? Did you really come just to see me? I'm not the only girl here, you know! Are you mad at me too?"

"You're concealing something from me!"

"According to you, I'm always concealing something from you."

"Well, aren't you? Did I ever scold you without a reason?"

His gorge was rising and he wanted the scolding to end.

"But if you don't like me this way, then why . . ."

"You mean why am I in love with you?"

She began to laugh in a way that was increasingly provocative.

"Would you like it if I weren't in love with you?" he demanded, his lips getting drier.

He was surprised at her silence. "I forgive you," he said. "Give me a kiss."

Slowly, modestly, almost as if she were afraid to grant him too much, she turned toward him. Then, just when they were about to kiss, she pulled away. Pietro was determined and forced her face up from where she was holding it down obstinately.

"Don't cry," he said.

He was afraid her inner lip was going to start quivering and the tears come gushing as though from an artesian well. "Listen to me," he said, hands still on her temples though speaking in a meeker, more desperate, almost pleading tone.

She looked up.

"Have you changed your mind about marrying me?"

She kept staring at him, then tried to blink back her tears in a way that usually worked. When she didn't cry, he was impressed.

He bent down and kissed her throat, made her look up, then gazed in her eyes as if enchanted.

"Why do you have to try to trick me?" he asked, his throat tight with repugnance and moral distaste.

She could tell he was suspicious and so she kept quiet.

Pietro took her face again, a face stiff as flint, turning it in his hands and forced her to look at him. She twisted like a lizard that turns and runs off.

"You were going to just disappear!"

Conceding this, she disentangled her hands and turned away.

He stared at her in embarrassment.

But she was afraid he might try to get even and smiled pliantly. Throwing his arms around her, he gave her a kiss.

"But I'm not the one you're in love with," she said.

"Why do you always say that?" he asked bewilderedly, pressing his body tight against her.

A cold sweat had suddenly come over him and he was trying to get calmer by touching her body. "So I'm not in love with you?" he demanded.

"You are going to marry someone else," she said calmly and without emotion.

The blood drained from his face and he had barely enough strength to totter to the door.

"Is this how you love me?" shouted Ghisola, trying to insult him.

Then, for the very first time, she gave him her mouth. He hesitated, but then let the drunkenness rush over him.

"Why were you pressing against me like that?" insisted Ghisola, who wanted him to take her so she could make him believe he had made her pregnant.

Pietro refused to answer. "I know why," Ghisola burst out. "I can guess. Now you've stopped because you want me too. You can't hold back any longer. Well if that's what you want, go ahead: I'm yours."

But then Lucia called out from the kitchen and they sat down to dinner. There were just the three of them since the sister's husband was out of town that day.

By two in the afternoon Pietro was explaining to Ghisola that he had to go back. But Ghisola had forgotten that he had to leave. "Sleep here," she cried happily.

"My father will be waiting. You know he'd make it worse for you too if I stayed!"

"Sleep here," Ghisola insisted. "I'll come and kiss you like that time in Siena."

By now he was concerned they might really be able to sleep together and so he refused.

"Aren't we with each other during the day without doing anything wrong?" asked Ghisola, guessing his thoughts.

"I swear you'll respect me," she went on innocently, "because you don't want for us . . ."

"No I don't. You have to be my wife first. If I say this to you it's because I love you."

Slamming the door, she left the room. Her flesh was so drenched with desire it was like a sponge soaked in oil. As Pietro hesitated whether to stay or leave, she came back.

"We can be together afterwards," he said in the same whiny tone she used. "For now we'll just have to be patient. We'll have to!"

"Answer me!" he insisted, taking her waist.

Feigning an ingenuousness so natural it would have fooled anyone, Ghisola hid her face in her apron.

"Why are you hiding your face? Stop it. I won't have it."

When they came downstairs, they were holding tight to each other's hand and she had such a timid and innocent air that he felt sorry and couldn't imagine how he could have scolded her.

At the bottom of the stairs, Ghisola leaned against the doorjamb. One foot in the road already, he was waiting for her to say something. When she didn't even seem to be thinking about him, he didn't add anything either. Instead he walked slowly away from town, though he was strongly tempted to turn and look back.

Rousing herself, Ghisola stared at where he had been standing. Then she put her hands against the doorjamb, pushed away off from it, and slipped back into the house.

She didn't say a word to her sister about Pietro.

For Ghisola, Pietro's love meant a greater consciousness of what she was doing. She had to betray him, she felt, or else be humiliated. The deeper and more irrational their love became, the more it was necessary to stay on her guard. It wasn't that she liked being this way or was trying to change the way she lived, just that she didn't want Pietro to learn everything. She wished she could control things and be accepted for what she was, since then she could feel he was part of that same guilt she couldn't quite shake off.

If she could get him to marry her, once she had the baby, she knew she could dominate him and make him believe whatever she wanted.

She was convinced she was better off now, and much more attractive too than when she was nothing but a silly peasant with terrible clothes. She could sense that she had become shrewder and more astute, though she was so self-centered she never imagined what a painful awakening was in store for Pietro.

The reason she was trying to take advantage was that he was so rich he could save her from what was becoming an increasingly insecure situation. It terrified her to think of growing old without having experienced any real affection. Her resistance to Pietro's insistence on her purity was thus transformed to a sort of hatred as she began to fear he was going to find out all about her.

His very ingenuousness, she sensed, was a serious obstacle: not just a failing that made her superior. Since there was no indication that Pietro's devoted (though unwittingly insulting) attitude was going to change, she could feel her own position getting weaker and weaker each day.

She was partially right in viewing him as conceited, because if he had an inkling of what was happening, he would never forgive her. This was why she disliked how he made love, though she never considered changing her ways even to escape that constant humiliation. All she did sense was a kind of regret; and it was finally this that made her feel some measure of affection for Pietro.

It must also be said that it never occurred to her that one way to make him understand was to explain everything right from the beginning!

She concluded instead that she still hadn't fooled him sufficiently to get him to take the blame for her pregnancy!

She also wanted to get even with Domenico; it gave her a cruel kind of pleasure to see his son so crazy about her!

Pietro's scruples, furthermore, were ridiculous: silly nonsense completely unheard of in a young man his age.

What was he looking for, anyway? Why had he fallen in love with her instead of somebody from Siena from his own social class?

She did have to take things seriously, however, for the sake of her grandparents and other relatives. She was being offered a chance to become a lady and live without working; this had to be considered too. Furthermore, she hadn't done anything to encourage Pietro, and Domenico had better not say anything about it! His son was the one taking advantage of her—just because she worked for them! And this was the son she was supposed to trust!

For all that, however, there was a lot she could remember about her life at Poggio a' Meli. She had come to like it and enjoyed going back and being flattered by the hands. Though the way they did it was a bit double-edged, since they made it quite clear they didn't trust her as much as Pietro, or even as much as Giacco and Masa, who by now were resigned to the situation.

Ever since that first evening at Radda when she came in and announced she was leaving and they should pay no attention to gossip because not a word of it was true, her parents didn't dare say anything.

But her parents were pleased to see her dressed better than even the mayor's daughter—and he was very rich. Her sisters were jealous and told themselves she was a lot cleverer than they were. All her other relatives were fond of her and immediately took her defense.

Borio was dead from pneumonia. His rival, the farm foreman, had grown old so fast that the two or three times he did see Ghisola, he lifted his hat blushing and spoke respectfully.

In town too, when the news spread that she was going to marry the son of the *The Blue Fish*'s owner, no one judged her very severely.

Naturally, everyone thought back about the old days, but only to laugh unmaliciously, even concluding that she had always been a good girl, though perhaps a bit wild. And everyone respected her needy parents.

But after her boyfriend left her, Ghisola began to be concerned.

She would think back often of her months at Badia a Ripoli where she had enjoyed her independence, yet could still be sure Signor Alberto would come home each night.

She had to live outside Florence, it was true, in the country almost, but she had everything she needed and could go to the city whenever she wanted, as long as someone went with her.

Her bedroom looked onto the same garden that had given Pietro such a fright; the dining room was on the street across from some vacant lots.

Instead of houses, there was a boundary wall here that was not quite as high as the wheat and a cypress tree that in summer was covered with bindweed. The top of the wall had been repaired with mortar and primroses and yellow rape weed grew on it.

In the distance a brook glistened where they washed their clothes, spreading them to dry in a meadow near a gate with two square pillars topped by a pair of terracotta dogs.

Dust from the road blew into the wheat and the cleaning rags hung out to dry billowed like the children's kites that sometimes blew over from Campo di Marte.

All she had to do when she wanted something from the fruit vendor was to lean out from the kitchen balcony and choose from the boxes displayed below. There was a grocer further up who also sold wine. When the wind was blowing from that direction, they got the smells from his shop too. Well-to-do clerks and their families and some kitchen gardeners lived in the other houses. But she kept to herself and no one was scandalized in the least.

By now she was walking the streets every day, but the deeper she sank and the filthier she got from that sort of life, the more she was able to appreciate Pietro, in part because she felt utterly unable, even for an hour, to live up to the ideal he had of her. The less important he became for her, the less she was troubled by the moral uneasiness that bothered her so the first few months.

By now she was that sort of a woman. Since giving it up would make little sense, she resigned herself more to her lot each day.

Her letters from Pietro made her think he was writing to some decent girl that he planned to marry. She would smile at this and feel sorry for him.

Though he knew full well he was wasting his time, Pietro went to Florence in September, using his make-up examinations as an excuse. He thought it fair and a proper punishment that he had to give up his books and his Sienese friends, who by now wouldn't even say hello. It was as though he was hiding, compromising himself with everyone. But he also had an urge to drop into the abyss and the feeling made his heart pump and swell in a way he had never experienced before!

Except to eat, he never left the building in Via Cimabue. Though he worried about this and wondered whether he should do something different, this was the way it had to be.

Ghisola had been in Florence for some time when he got there. She was installed in one of the so-called houses and was making a good deal of money. When a letter from Pietro was forwarded from

Radda, she went straight to see him in the hopes she could keep him from suspecting the truth.

His landlady admitted her and was going to call him. But Ghisola motioned not to bother, slipped over, and knocked with her fingertips on the door to his room. Guessing who it was, he leaped to his feet and threw open the door.

Ghisola pretended she didn't want to go in. Trembling violently, he pulled her inside and kissed her.

"I don't want to do that any more," she said, smiling and twisting.

She took off her hat, put it on her knees, and sat down.

But he felt such a hot surge in his heart that he couldn't help asking, flushing as he did, "Why did you leave Radda without even writing?"

"I just got here," she said, heedless of what she was saying but with that face of hers that was sometimes suffused by an absolute purity. "The lady I worked for at Badia a Ripoli made me come back. And there was no one in Radda to write you a letter because I didn't want anyone to know that we're lovers. Did I do right?"

"Yes you did. Is she taking you back?"

"Yes."

"I'm glad. But can't you at least spend today with me?"

"I've already got the permission."

He believed this and, in a burst of gratitude, threw his arms around her.

They immediately went out for a walk through Florence, had something to eat, and then stopped to talk on one of those benches in the Piazza San Marco where soldiers and idlers buy pumpkin seeds and anise cookies.

"I have to go now," she said with a laugh in the evening. "If I'm late getting back, I won't be able to come out again."

And so they parted—he without thinking to check which way she was going.

For the next three days he stayed in his room waiting for her, thinking he would tell her about his exams, and wondering if Ghisola cared anything about them. The thought filled him with a pleasure that was almost voluptuous.

Noises, even slight ones, had become unbearable and he could only avoid them by falling to sleep on his bed. His temples would throb less then and he wouldn't notice if his heart swelled up. But it worried and frightened him that his hands were cold and he was reminded of life in Siena.

If he weren't afraid that Ghisola wouldn't like it, he would have mustered all the sweetness that he felt at the notion and begged her to kill them both.

But everything changed when Ghisola visited. Even if she said he was crazy, or laughed in his face with that terrifying laugh that made her more beautiful—it still wouldn't matter!

They spent another day like the first one together; it was the last time they saw each other this way.

Pietro pretended, when he got back to Siena, that the exams had gone badly.

He was becoming convinced that he was the victim of injustices that people should unite and resist together.

"What have you done?" Domenico shouted. "Why didn't you study more? Can't you see you're not cut out for school?"

As long as Ghisola wasn't a part of it, Domenico's anger seemed reasonable.

Before long, Pietro's ill-humor and anxiety reappeared. Since his love had increased for Ghisola, this time it was worse than ever. Nothing else touched or even seemed to concern him.

He felt as though he had fallen into a void and wasn't able to scramble out. Was it Ghisola's fault? Of course not: it was only his own, and he was embarrassed to face her. "If it weren't for Ghisola, I'd kill myself," he would muse waking up in the morning. He could feel the moral tranquillity of earlier days begin slipping away.

For a little while, Domenico did not not let on that he was impatient for Pietro to get involved in the business. But their conversations were starting to have that air of forced politeness that conceals angry undercurrents and they started to avoid even talking. Everyone was expecting a battle and hurried to take Rosi's side. Pietro knew what was happening and pretended not to understand the furtive glances his father was casting his way. Sometimes Domenico would persuade himself that he was a rough, simple man threatened by a wicked and sophisticated enemy. And then he would worry he was going to lose.

What good were his efforts, a whole life of labor? Wasn't he going to take all he had won with astuteness and hard work and turn it over to his son when he died? How could the boy not understand? Did he want to ruin his inheritance?

He realized how mistaken he had been to give him so much freedom in the Ghisola matter. And he had brought her into the house himself! And now, the slut, she was turning his own son away and making him hate him!

It seemed an elaborate plot: seminary, art school, technical school, technical institute, private teachers, everything!

He had thought so much about this, it was impossible for him to back down now.

Seated on a chair that had served him twenty years or more, hands in his trousers and leaning his already bald head on the wall, he kept his eye on Pietro. But he didn't say anything and tried to turn his mind elsewhere by chatting with the help or greeting the customers.

Pietro was dreaming of the family treasures that he and Ghisola would own one day.

He thought about the quiet, even-burning lamp with the milk-glass shade; his mother's chair with the drawer beneath the backrest where she kept her wool skeins and the pair of penny novels that were her only books; the four pillows, each misshapen in its own way, that she used for her back; the smell of her cologne; her smelling salts; her little worn gold cross.

Lying in his hard bed waiting for sleep, he would think about all the familiar objects and the intense, inarticulate affection he felt for them. Ghisola was going to renew everything and he felt it necessary to assign new importance and significance to them. That same sweetness he felt when he was with her again rolled over him.

When the candle was gone, he turned to the wall and went to sleep.

Toward midnight, Domenico walked through his bedroom, a brass lantern in his hand. Pietro woke and was going to lift his head, but the other door went shut, leaving him annoyed the way it happens when a certain mood is interrupted.

Early the next morning, Domenico left. He said nothing to Pietro, who lay in bed trying to give a different shading to the dreams that arrive between sleeping and waking when it seems we can choose to wake up or keep dreaming.

Scrunching his knees, he sat down idly at his desk. It wasn't possible for things to be so indifferent while his sensual memory was reaching a state of crazy excitement.

As he saw it, it was his destiny to suffer, and this moved him deeply. "Why can't I see Ghisola? Nobody has to give up things the way I do. And no one else gets so confused, either. I can't understand how people do so many things that I could never manage. The coachman, for example, when he whips his horse to make it run faster, or the streetcleaner who sprinkles the streets with water."

He was careful, however, to avoid the restaurant until time for dinner. Even then, he had to choose his moment or be barked at by the cook; he had to be satisfied with whatever they gave him and got his own bread and cutlery from the pantry.

Though he had once had high ideals of love for humanity, he felt only a bitter disappointment now.

"Stay out of the way when the waiters are passing," his father would say. "You aren't working here!"

In order to avoid being given some work, he would leave the restaurant. "Do they really expect me to trot over to the grocer's for cheese? Or take a basket and fill it with bread? Or argue with somebody about his bill? If that were the case, Ghisola wouldn't want me."

One day a letter arrived. It was clear immediately from the writing on the envelope that something inevitable had come to pass. At first he refused to open it. But when he did, he read, "Ghisola is betraying you. For further proof, go to Via della Pergola . . ."

A house number and a woman's name—both false no doubt—came next.

The words seemed to dispel a vague worry of some sort. "There has to be an explanation," he thought.

All kinds of painful, troubling thoughts began to race through his head. But it also astounded him that a stranger had felt such compassion.

He wondered how to get the money he needed to go and surprise Ghisola. Rebecca wasn't willing to loan him any more, complaining that he hadn't paid her back for the last time.

"How can you expect me to ask my father?" he insisted.

"Ask a friend."

She wanted to prove that her niece was innocent and had already decided to give him the money. While they were talking she moved toward the bureau. But first she got a clean diaper for the baby she was carrying and spread it on the bed, throwing the dirty one under the wardrobe and pretending that the child's squalling had driven thoughts of money out of her head.

Head down, she appeared to be thinking. If she had believed it would do any good, she was ready to talk to Domenico herself. But there was no sense getting involved just for Pietro!

"Can't you wait and go in the morning?" she asked.

"Is that possible after a letter like this?" he replied.

She understood and gave a sigh.

"Give it here," he said in a moment.

"How much do you need?"

"More than last time."

"Where am I supposed to get it for God's sake! Why don't you try to put a little aside each week?"

It exasperated him to think this had never occurred to him, though he couldn't imagine why it hadn't.

"From now on, I will. This time . . . you give it to me."

Had he been made to wait much longer, he would have given up. But Rebecca was persuaded and agreed.

She leaned back against the open drawer, staring into his face as Pietro counted the money. He smiled and thanked her.

"Mind you give it back," she cautioned from the landing.

Even if her mail had been forwarded to Badia a Ripoli, couldn't she have moved just a few days earlier? What was it all about?

He tried to imagine what might have happened. Since none of the possibilities seemed very likely, he gave up trying to evaluate them. It seemed likely, for once, that the melancholy circumstances that had been accumulating were so far off that he could get rid of them. All his troubles seemed external ones and he even felt a twinge of happiness unlike anything he had experienced before. "Why did I believe that letter so quickly?" he thought.

During the trip he was practically unconscious, as though gripped by a fever, but at the same time he was extremely impatient to arrive.

The train rushed alongside the Arno where the water was sparkling so brightly it seemed thousands of mirrors were crashing to pieces. It sped past sheer, bristly pine forests dotted with violet shadows, past telegraph poles in front of trembling white poplars, past clumps of cypresses nearly concealed by additional trees. On it went toward the city where a gentle blue was gathering above and between hills whose outline was becoming softer and softer. The sight of such stupendous beauty humiliated him. Even though he couldn't understand it, the love he had for Ghisola till now suddenly seemed an abominable indignity. "Could it be possible I shouldn't love her?"

He went in through the door indicated in the letter, passing some women who refused to make a passage for him. The stairs were filthy and dark and smelled of sweat and face powder.

A door was ajar on the second floor. Through it he caught sight of a prostitute dressed in a crimson wrapper; she gave him a look that was almost sarcastic.

Another apartment on the third floor was open. Stopping to listen, he heard women's voices and merriment; one woman was singing softly. He explained this to himself first in the worst, then in the best possible way. But a shudder came over him. "How could Ghisola be living with people like this?" And he dashed up the remaining stairs as if pursued.

On the top floor, he halted, out of breath. Though his vision was growing foggy, he could tell that he was in a parlor that had an oval table in the center. Vaguely and indistinctly, he began to make out a woman on a couch; she was talking to a soldier whose cap lay on a chair close by.

Pietro was staring in great agitation and this alarmed the woman. She tapped the soldier's knee and they both turned to look. When he stepped forward, it was as though his legs had disappeared. He seemed face to face with a sudden nightmare whose existence he refused to acknowledge. He stammered something. When the woman didn't answer, he concluded he must have offended her and started to move off. Just then, Ghisola came through the door. When she saw him, she stopped immediately and turned so pale she almost fainted. Then she stepped backwards, leaning on the wall with one elbow, like a mouse that is trying to escape after being half-crushed by a blow.

Determined not to give in to the total disorientation that had come over him, and sensing that some strange force was dragging him forward, Pietro staggered after her into a room where all he could see was the window.

By the time he got there she had taken off her dirty jacket and was sitting where he couldn't see the swell of her pregnancy.

"What are you doing here?" he said, close to tears and bending to kiss her.

She didn't know what to answer. "Has he noticed I'm pregnant? How can I tell him? I knew this would happen."

"Nobody lives here but women," she said.

Suddenly he no longer believed her. "I won't have it," he answered. "Get dressed. What's this bruise on your arm?"

She was afraid she wouldn't remember her story. "I bit myself," she answered.

He thought that maybe she was telling the truth. Then, after a long moment when he hoped that everything would just disappear, he said, "Let's get out of here. I want to talk to you."

"We're staying right here. I'm not going anywhere today."

Another pause followed. "Why didn't I find out what kind of betrayal the letter meant?" he wondered. "This way I'll never know anything for certain. What am I going to say?"

"I don't like this place. What sort of place is it?"

"I'll explain everything. There's nothing wrong with it."

She had decided several times to tell him she was pregant, but was so surprised that she couldn't say anything and was doing her best to hide the whole matter. He felt he should hurry and say what he wanted.

"Get up."

The owner of the establishment came in. A strong, husky woman with a white leather belt, she was a midwife more than capable of restraining her patients when they thrashed around during labor.

The effect of what he had said further intimidated Pietro. He turned to explain why he was there. The woman, who knew everything, could see no way out for Ghisola and was worried he was going to kill her.

Ghisola, in a burst of hysteria that her condition made even stronger, was staring at the window, ready to fling herself from it.

The woman hung back, straightening out the washstand and folding up a towel, one eye on Pietro and the other on Ghisola. She was looking for an indication of what she should do.

Pietro, growing more impatient at her every move, was waiting for her to go. Finally, making an effort, he announced, "I'd like to be alone with Ghisola."

In the meantime, without getting up or letting him notice, Ghisola had changed her blouse. "Go ahead. . ." she answered. "I'll take care of things."

She was utterly terrified, afraid that in a moment she would have to fall on her knees.

The woman went out reluctantly, leaving the door unlocked, and lurking behind it to listen. Pietro had noticed and wanted to lock the door before he demanded an explanation. But he couldn't turn the key. He still didn't want to hurt Ghisola and would gladly have postponed the entire encounter.

"Don't lock it," she said, getting up. "No one can hear us."

At this, eyes filled with pity and affection, he turned and saw her belly.

When Pietro came to after the violent dizziness that had flung him at Ghisola's feet, he realized that he no longer loved her.

Translator's Afterword

Tozzi's Life

Federigo Tozzi was born in Siena on New Year's Day, 1883, the same year as Kafka. His father, Federigo, or "Ghigo," was an unusually irascible and tyrannical man. Of peasant stock, the elder Tozzi was the proprietor of a flourishing restaurant called "Il Sasso" or "The Rock," and was known in Siena as "Ghigo del Sasso," a nickname as descriptive of his character as of his occupation. Tozzi's mother, Annunziata, was a foundling and of fragile constitution, suffering among other things from attacks of epilepsy—very likely the unnamed malady that also afflicts Pietro in *Ghisola*. Like the Rosi's in *Ghisola*, the Tozzi family was a tense one; the emotional storms between the frail and sensitive son, the rough-hewn father, and the remissive doting mother that battered it are faithfully reproduced in the novel, often down to the last humiliating detail. For at least in its main outlines, there seems to be very little fiction in *Ghisola*. Apparently, Tozzi's father really did regard his namesake and only surviving offspring as some sort of changeling, a living and odious refutation of his style and identity. This is evident from the letters in *Novale* documenting the physical and verbal abuse ("You're no son of mine . . . You're a degenerate . . . a coward") that Ghigo heaped on his son. Though the gentle Annunziata was able to mitigate some of this violence, when she died in 1895 the future writer suffered deeply from the shock.

At school the young Tozzi's experiences were just as turbulent and frustrating as at home. Expelled from the local seminary for low grades and poor deportment, Tozzi was to steer an irregular course from one institution of learning to another, a course that finally ran

143

completely aground when he failed his exams in drawing and Italian and was forbidden to continue at the technical college. Blocked in his attempts at formal study, Tozzi set out to educate himself in the Biblioteca Comunale of Siena. Here his only authority was that of his own intellectual appetites, his only limits those that were set by his own capacities and the library's holdings. A self-educated person, Tozzi learned what he knew in isolation from university circles or the sophisticated cultural and artistic milieu that nearby Florence, for example, might have provided. For this reason, perhaps, his life-long attitude toward Italy's intellectual and cultural establishment was one of unremitting truculence.

Toward the end of 1902, the same year he failed his technical school exams, Tozzi responded to an ad in the lonely hearts column of a local newspaper. In doing this he was plunging "with his eyes closed" into a passionate correspondance with a woman who at once became his confidante and later his wife. The selections from her husband's letters published by Emma Palagi Tozzi in 1925 as *Novale* are important not only for their moving description of the couple's love, but also for a description of a fervid, though one-sided, emotional entanglement between the young Tozzi and a peasant girl from his father's farm: the first glimmerings of the later *Ghisola.*

In 1907, bolstered emotionally and financially by the unwavering Emma, Tozzi left Siena for Rome and a career in journalism. But when the capital proved less than welcoming to the aspiring writer, Tozzi went to work as a railroad clerk. He was assigned to Pontedera, a town not too far from Siena. But when the elder Federigo died, in May of 1908, he hurried back to Siena and quickly married Emma.

The restaurant and two farms Tozzi inherited from his father should have guaranteed a comfortable living for many years. But Ghigo's "Rock" was tied up in his son's mind with the poisonous relations between him and his father. Quickly—more quickly than prudently—Federigo sold the restaurant. He also sold one of the farms, going to live at the other: "Il Castagneto" or "The Chestnut Grove," the model for the Poggio a' Meli so rapturously described in the novel. For even though the properties Federigo had inherited from Ghigo were weighted down with complicated and obscure legal entanglements, the years Tozzi spent in the country were the happiest and most productive of his life. It was during this period from 1908 to 1914 that he wrote most of his more important works: completing *Ghisola* and the *Ricordi di un impiegato* ("Memoirs of a Clerk," based on his experiences in Pontedera); writing a first draft of *Il podere* ("The Farm"); and turning out a large number of essays, poems, and short stories, including the prose sketches of *Bestie* ("Animals"), the collection that launched his career when it was published by Treves in 1917.

Like Remigio in *Il podere*, who is so inept at running a farm inherited from his father that an enraged peasant murders him, Tozzi was not an able steward of Ghigo's property. By 1914 he was so broke that he rented out the remaining farm and went back to Rome to try again as a journalist; but even though Italy had not yet joined the hostilities, Tozzi quickly found that the eve of the Great War was, as Emma put it, "no time for literature." After working as press aide for the Italian Red Cross, in 1918 Tozzi was taken on by a Rome weekly. In 1919 he published *Con gli occhi chiusi*, his first novel. In the same year he finished *Il podere* and wrote all of *Tre croci* ("Three Crosses")—a tale of debts and suicide and his only non-autobiographical novel. Then, in March of 1920, not long after the publication of *Con gli occhi chiusi*, and just as *Il podere* and *Tre croci* were coming off the presses, Tozzi died of pneumonia—the result, some biographers assert, of having slept with the window open. He was 37. Although treated at first with only passing interest as an eccentric figure of mostly regional importance, more recent critical thought considers Tozzi one of the founders (along with Svevo and Pirandello) of the modern Italian novel.

The Translation

Tozzi's prose, while always clear and frequently beautiful, is an anomaly in the tradition of Italian expository writing as exemplified by such writers as Machiavelli, Tasso, Leopardi, or Croce. What makes his work so different from these masters of lucid and balanced exposition is its idiosyncratic syntax—or rather lack of syntax. Unlike most of his predecessors in Italian prose, Tozzi organizes his thoughts and impressions linearly rather than hierarchically; his style is thus predominantly paratactic rather than syntactic. On the level of sentence construction, this means a preference for the simple copula "and" and "but" between independent clauses rather than for subordination and the hierarchy it implies. On the level of plot, Tozzi's writing is also paratactic in its presentation of bits of action side by side without narrative subordination or indication of relative importance and by a penchant for sometimes startling temporal leaps and illogical concatenations of sentences, paragraphs, and episodes.

This preference for parataxis over syntax and linear over hierarchical narrative structures is particularly evident in *Ghisola*. In this novel Tozzi describes impressions from the external world beating on a sensibility too baffled by their impact to be able to impose any order, attribution of cause and effect, or meaning on the stimuli that buffet and bewilder him. In this chronicle of an almost pathologically sensitive adolescent during a crucial moment of his existence, Tozzi is more concerned with how Pietro Rosi's sensorium reacts to the various impressions that thrash against it than with such extrinsic issues as the kinds or degree of social importance that these impressions imply. This is why Pietro's responses to meteorological conditions or the incandescent flora and fauna that sometimes besiege him are just as important as his struggles with his father or his intense and frustrating relationship with Ghisola.

In my attempt to render Tozzi's eccentrically organized and idiosyncratically punctuated prose into English, I have not found it desirable to follow his paratactic methods strictly, at least not at the level of the sentence. In the interests of readability, I have not hesitated to change his original syntax by transposing clauses, altering the original punctuation (abandoning Tozzi's beloved but bizarrely employed semicolon, for example, in favor of more conventional marks), and introducing a greater sense of causality than is always the case in the original. Tozzi's most frequently used conjunction, for example—not only in this novel, but throughout his works—is probably the adversative "ma," which I have as often rendered "although" or "since" as "but," "however," "nevertheless," and so on.

Another element of Tozzi's style that is lost in translation is his special lexicon. A Tuscan, and a self-educated and fiercely independent one at that, Tozzi was enormously proud of his provincial linguistic heritage. He had absorbed this tradition not only from the speech he heard daily in the Sienese streets and countryside, but also from the writings of the medieval Sienese Saints Catherine and

Bernardino, whose works he edited in two notable anthologies: *Antologia d'antichi scrittori senesi* and *Le cose più belle di Santa Caterina da Siena*. Derived as it is from both the local dialect and the written canon, Tozzi's language is at once rustic and literary, intellectual and countrified, bookish and unlettered, archaic and contemporary— a unique instance in modern Italian literature.

A final word should be said about the title. In the draft accepted by the publisher, Tozzi's novel was called *Ghisola*, just as it is in this translation. It was only after acceptance by Treves that Tozzi decided to give it the title *Con gli occhi chiusi*, a phrase that means "with eyes closed" and thus "blindly" or "headlong," with connotations of both the passive shutting out of visual reality and the blind impetuosity that alternately characterize Pietro's interactions with the world. Despite its aptness as a description of Pietro's problematic relation with reality, I have not been able to find an English equivalent for this phrase. For this reason, I have decided to return to the original *Ghisola* as a title for this translation. In doing so, I draw consolation from the notion that Tozzi's concern that a woman's name would make his book seem "too much a 'romanzo per signorine'" hardly seems justified today.

A novel for "signorine"—a phrase Tozzi meant to describe readers of whatever sex who require titillation, evasion, and a consolatory conclusion from fiction—*Ghisola* certainly is not. A violent work on several different levels—syntactic, narrative, sexual, familial, cosmic—it is very much a product of that turbulent period in Italian history that historians have dubbed "the suicide of the liberal state" and that witnessed the first stirrings of what would later be Fascism. At the same time, this is a novel of more than documentary value, a work whose richness and universality make it an appropriate object for reflection at other moments in the history of our times.

Conclusion

Ghisola is an unusual love story. It is a reflection on the imponderable, on the inalienable, on the vice of growth. And it is also a dictionary of poetical speculations, of real dolorous and irreplaceable facts. Tozzi wrote it when he was in his mid-twenties. Except for the painters of his native Siena and the writings of his fellow Sienese Saints Catherine and Bernardino, he knew very little about art and literature. If Tozzi's writings are emaciated and intense, reduced to essentials like the Madonnas of the Sienese painters who lived before Petrarch and seem to look beyond their remote grace, there is no doubt that this is due to the tremendous psychic influence that Siena had on him. But like the Sienese Madonnas, Tozzi's Siena is also remote and immaterial ("abstract" as the writer Corrado Alvaro put it), and it is only against this abstract background that his characters move.

From today's perspective we may say that Tozzi was metaphysically ill, part of the same family of "misfits" as Kafka or Artaud, Julian Green or Adamov—all writers who looked out upon existence from physical and intellectual prisons and finally reduced the terms of the quotidian to its ultimate consequences. Tozzi's *angst* was made up of a desire for self-affirmation and recognition, anxiety to communicate, an obsession with sex, mental disturbances, imaginary dread, doubt, and, finally, a collapse of reason—an *angst* that separated the "I" from the "world."

The solitary and dogged work that he produced has resulted in a highly moral teaching regarding the courage to live, which is also the courage to create, especially for those who, at one moment or another of their human and intellectual history, have felt the cruel blows of despair and failure, negation and exile, and who have nonetheless renounced surrender. Federigo Tozzi is an opaque pearl in twentieth-century Italian literature. His *Con gli occhi chiusi* is a masterpiece; *Ghisola*, its excellent English translation, should help him to rise in all his fullness and importance from the shadows where he has been so unjustly cast.

Some Titles in the Series

JAMES J. WILHELM
General Editor

9. Ramón Hernández, *Invitation to Die.*
   Translated from Spanish by Marion Freeman.

10. Edvard Hoem, *The Ferry Crossing.*
    Translated from New Norwegian by
    Frankie Denton Shackelford.

11. Henrik Ibsen, *"Catiline" and "The Burial Mound."*
    Translated from Dano-Norwegian by Thomas Van Laan.

12. Banabhatta, *Kadambari: A Classic Sanskrit Story of Magical
    Transformations.* Translated from Sanskrit by
    Gwendolyn Layne.

13. *Selected Poetry of Lina Kostenko.*
    Translated from Ukrainian by Michael Naydan.

14. Baptista Mantuanus, *Adulescentia: The Eclogues of Mantuan.*
    Translated from Latin by Lee Piepho.

15. *The Mourning Songs of Greek Women.*
    Translated from Greek by Konstantinos Lardas.

16. *Ono no Komachi: Poems, Stories, and Noh Plays.*
    Translated from Japanese by Roy E., Nicholas J.,
    and Helen Rebecca Teele.

17. Adam Small, *Kanna—He Is Coming Home.*
    Translated from Afrikaans by Carrol Lasker.

18. Federigo Tozzi, *Ghisola.*
    Translated from Italian by Charles Klopp.

19. *Women Poets in Russia: The Burden of Sufferance.*
    Translated from Russian by Albert Cook and Pamela Perkins.

20. Chantal Chawaf, *Mother Love, Mother Earth.*
    Translated from French by Monique Nagem.